THE BOY WITH THE GOLDEN SURFBOARD

The Big Feller was a monster that had voyaged from the very heart of the ocean five thousand miles away from shore. It had brute force that scared me more than I had ever been scared before. The wave hoisted me up on to its crest and bustled me away. It was so right, was this wave, and by a fluke my timing was right.

No ski, surfboard, speedboat, hydrofoil, jet plane or interplanetary rocket could have given me such a feeling of speed, power, and thrust.

The ride seemed to last for an hour, a day, a week. It ended when the gallant wave conquered the beach and left me in a glad, limp heap in the shallowest of shallow water.

'Wunderbar!' said Jiranek.

'Marvelloso!' I said.

The Boy with the Golden Surfboard

David Bateson

CAROUSEL EDITOR: ANNE WOOD

CAROUSEL BOOKS
A DIVISION OF TRANSWORLD PUBLISHERS LTD
A NATIONAL GENERAL COMPANY

THE BOY WITH THE GOLDEN SURFBOARD
A CAROUSEL BOOK 0 552 52030 6

First publication in Great Britain

PRINTING HISTORY
Carousel edition published 1973

Copyright © David Bateson 1973
Copyright © Illustrations Transworld Publishers Ltd. 1973

Carousel Books are published by Transworld Publishers Ltd.,
Cavendish House, 57–59 Uxbridge Road, Ealing, London W.5

Made and printed in Great Britain by
Richard Clay (The Chaucer Press), Ltd., Bungay, Suffolk.

**NOTE: The Australian price appearing on the
back cover is the recommended retail price.**

For
JO DIANE

ONE

GOOFY-FOOTER

Ever heard of a goofy-footer? I'm one.

A goofy-footer is a surfer who has his right foot forward when he's riding a surfboard, the way a southpaw boxer stands.

'That's doing things the wrong way round,' somebody tells me.

But I say: 'I throw left-handed. I hold my pencil left-handed. So this is the proper way for me.'

And I blow them a raspberry.

In a sense, my Dad is the same. He goes about things in a different way from other people. Especially Mum.

For a year Mum had been saying about the migrant hostel: 'It's time we got away from here and found a place of our own ... or went back to the old country.'

Well I didn't want to go all the way back over the ocean to the smoke of the blast furnaces where I had started my life. So I hoped Mum would help us to get a place of our own in Sydney. She didn't.

Then one day Dad came back to the hostel and said: 'It's all fixed. Loan payments. Everything.

We're shifting.'

'Shifting!' breathed Mum. 'Where to?'

'Bondi Beach,' said Dad. He was an ex-sailor, but worked in a dockyard now, and wanted to be where he could breath the clean salt air of the Pacific. 'Tumbledown old place, but at Bondi, who cares?'

'Wow!' I cheered. 'That's the place to go!'

'I'd rather move into a modern small house in one of the smart new suburbs,' said Mum cautiously.

'Oh, no,' I begged. 'Make it Bondi Beach for me.'

'Or Luna Park,' said Clare. She's my sister, a few years younger but just as goofy-minded.

'You can't live in an amusement park, Clare,' Mum told her.

'But you can live at Bondi Beach,' I insisted. 'There's the surf . . . and there's the sand, tons and tons and tons of it.'

'All right,' agreed Clare, 'make it Bondi Beach.'

'Mum, you're outvoted three to one,' I snorted.

I knew that Mum didn't like the tumbledown little house Dad had picked out near the beach. She wanted something clean and modern, like the new ones on the other side of the city.

'But it's not only that,' she protested.

'What then?' asked Dad.

'Yes, what then?' I said.

'A feeling I have,' she said distantly, with a frown creasing up the smooth fair skin on her forehead. 'A feeling about living near the beach.'

'What feeling, Mum?' I argued.

'Nothing . . . I'll not talk about it.'

'What feeling?' Dad pressed.

'All right,' said Mum, 'I'll tell you. I have a feeling something terrible is going to happen to us if we go and live near the beach.'

'Aw, nuts,' I said. 'The beach is just great.'

'Nothing terrible will happen,' said Dad. 'You'll see.'

Mum didn't say anything else about it just then. But later her words were:

'All right, I'll go and live near the beach. But under protest.'

So we moved house in the springtime.

We piled all our junk into an old meat truck that Dad had rented, then away it went from the hostel with us kids on top. It rumbled and spluttered through the early quietness of the city streets, all the way to Bondi Beach.

Goodbye to the place where we had spent the first part of our lives in New South Wales. Hello to the clear sky and the rolling blue waves and the spanking white surf and the silver sand.

We unloaded all our junk. We put it in the house where he had come to live, then wiped the sweat off our necks and went down near the beach to cool off.

'Take a look at that sun, Greg,' Dad told me, with a grin bright enough to match the morning light.

'No, Greg,' said Mum, 'don't look at the sun, or you, Clare.'

'I meant the sunshine, not the sun itself,' said Dad.

Clare screwed up her eyes and teased Mum, pretending to look directly at the sun.

'Brighter than a million searchlights, it is,' I said.

It wasn't always like that at Bondi. Sometimes there were clouds, and the ocean was grey, and there was no surf.

Sometimes there were arguments with other kids. Fights, even.

The time is going to come when I will have forgotten the arguments and the fights and the days without surf. But I shall never forget that first great day when we moved in.

After visiting Bondi Beach from the hostel I was already crazy about the surf there. I wanted to be a surf champion when I was old enough.

Trouble was, I didn't even own a real surfboard, fibreglass style.

'One day I'm going to have my own board,' I boasted. 'It's got to be a brand new board, one that nobody else has ever ridden.'

Mum flopped down in a chair, exhausted. She had been slaving in the house, making the place as spick and span as possible. 'You'll just have to wait, Greg,' she soothed. 'Surfboards are a lot of money, and too dangerous at your age.'

'I don't know about dangerous,' muttered Dad, 'but they're certainly a lot of money.'

Money always seemed to be cropping up in conversations between my parents.

Some people might have got the wrong idea about our finances, with us going to live at a famous spot like Bondi Beach. It sounds like the ultimate in luxury.

But there was very little luxury about our house. To find it you had to turn your back on the silver sand and the surf. You had to move away from the lush green grass in the park near the promenade, and that beautiful flood of rich sunlight, then go past the smart hotels and the bright restaurants smelling of fried bream and lamb chops and hamburgers. Eventually, like in most seaside places, you would come across a shabby street where the houses were not so fashionable.

One of those sad-faced houses belonged to us now. Its purply bricks were short of plaster and the paint was coming off the window frames in shreds. Inside the house you could see cracks in the ceiling and cracks in the wall.

'But,' said Dad when Mum complained about these, 'you have to admit it's a good thing there are a few cracks around the place.'

I was puzzled. 'How come, Dad?' I asked.

The laughter wrinkles puckered up on his sun-browned face. 'Well, Greg,' he said through a grin, 'don't you see that if this house didn't have all these cracks in it, we couldn't have afforded to buy it at all?'

Mum did not grin. The wrinkles around her eyes were mostly from worry. She shook her head slowly from side to side while talking, looking disappointed with the whole venture. Her voice sounded heavy with sadness. 'For less money than this, and without any borrowing difficulties, we could have been buying a brand new fibro house. No cracks in the ceiling, and no cracks in the walls.'

Clare, my little sister, looked up from her doll 'You mean a nice fibro house near the beach, Mum?' she piped up.

Like me, Clare was mad about the beach, though for different reasons. Paradise to her meant playing in the sand, or splashing through those little rock pools at the north end of the bay. There was a Milky Way of freckles all over her face because of all the hours she spent in the sun.

'You'd never get a house like that near the beach for this, would you?' I said.

'The beach, the beach, the beach,' said Mum. 'That's all I hear about these days. There are other places on earth apart from the beach, Greg.'

'Like where?' I said sulkily.

'Like new smart homes on tidy estates in a really up-to-date suburb.'

'Oh, sure,' said Dad, 'I know the ones you're talking about. Like pretty coloured boxes. About twenty or thirty miles from the beach.'

'Good for the children to grow up in,' argued Mum. 'With a decent kitchen, and a spotless bathroom—not a dark poky one like there is here.'

'But,' he said, 'the air in summer would be like the inside of a bakehouse, and that's not my kind of paradise.'

'And this isn't mine.'

Good old Dad for holding out, I thought. Apart

from the sheer excitement of living near the beach, there seemed to be something so very Australian about spending your time at Bondi—and to me that meant a lot.

So they'd go on arguing for a while, then Dad would say: 'I'm going for a beer.'

With him this was just talk. Other men would mean it if they said it. Not Dad. He would just go and park himself on a seat along Campbell Parade and stare at the ocean for an hour or so.

Like me he loved the ocean. He'd travelled all over the world, had Dad, and spent years along the Pacific coast of California. He had a deep healthy colour that enriched his skin.

'This is what I've always promised myself, Greg,' he told me. 'To settle down near the beach and spend some time listening to the ocean. To see those big ships come ploughing in towards the Heads, any day of the week. It's good to be somewhere like this, somewhere that a bloke like me can sit and dream his dreams . . .'

The ocean was good. The water was still cool in the early springtime but there was a promise of warmth to come.

I was glad about Dad and his dreams. Don't let's leave the beach, I thought. Don't let's ever leave the beach.

Dad was ten years older than Mum, but in lots of ways he seemed younger. I knew that once the chill left the water he'd go out in the surf now and again, splashing about just as eagerly as I did.

The weeks passed. The sun at noon looked so

much higher, and began to whip some heat into the ocean. Out came the warm-weather surfies to join the wet-suit boy's who had been out in the icy water.

Just about that time I found myself a mate called Sam Rukovski. The two of us were in the same grade at the old school along the beachfront, and we were both left-handed.

Sam was a Polish Jew. He was quicker than I was at arithmetic, and he was also quicker to put up his fists if he thought someone was trying to poke fun at him. My Dad said that Sam had inherited this from his parents because of the way they had been kicked about when they were young in Warsaw.

The trouble was that he was scared of the water. He would stay around the edge, looking shivery and miserable.

'Come in, Sam,' I would say. 'It won't hurt a bit.'

'Drop dead,' said Sam. 'We're not between the flags here. It's not safe.'

He was right. I had been long enough in Australia to know that you had to swim in the part where the beach guards stuck the warning flags. Then you were clear of the rip which could swish you out to sea in a flash, and you were also out of the way of the surfboards.

So I said:

'O.K., Sam, you're right this time. We can move along a bit and swim between the flags.'

But Sam Rukovski was a wily individual. Even

15

when we moved to the safe zone he stayed in the shallow part.

'It's more fun here,' he said.

'Come on, Sam,' I nagged, 'I'll teach you how to body-surf. Make you feel like a real Aussie.'

'Get lost,' he told me. His skin was normally a kind of a olive colour, but now it went the pale shade you go when you're chickening out on something.

'Try, boy, try.'

'Nuts, Greg. Anyway, you're no more a full-blooded Aussie than I am.'

I winced. 'No matter. I can teach you fine, anyway.'

'My father can teach me.'

That was a laugh. Sam's father had a game leg from being knocked around in the Second World War. He couldn't have swum the width of a cup of coffee. 'Last chance, Sam.'

'No.' He just stared out towards Ben Buckler, the nobbly headland at the north end of the beach.

'All right, Sammy,' I said. 'You please yourself, but I'm going to take a trip out into the Big Fellers.'

The Big Fellers were those hefty breakers that came tumbling along the shelf of moving sand along the bay, especially when the off-shore breezes blew. Dad had shown me how to enjoy myself in them. You ran the first few steps into the water, then flung yourself forward in a kind of flat dive through a broken wave.

You romped forward again, then dived through

the next broken wave, and so on—until you were able to stand on the ridge of sand.

Now you were neck-deep in the water and a fair distance from the shore. You were in the part where the incoming waves were about to froth up ready for breaking.

Sometimes you just bobbed up and down on the tips of your toes to keep your head in the air. Other times you needed to swim a stroke or two.

Now you were one of a group of body-surfers of all ages and sizes and abilities. There you were, all looking out at the Pacific, waiting for a Big Feller that would curl up high at the right moment to give you a ride towards the shore.

You could afford to be choosy. You could let a few go past you till the best ones came.

'If a wave hasn't broken, go over it,' Dad had told me. 'If it has broken, go through it or you'll get belted off your feet. Turn a bit sideways while you're waiting, then the water will glide past you better. But whatever you do, never turn your back on a real Big Feller.'

I had forgotten this rule a couple of times. Then I was punished, not by Dad but by the surf itself. It had thumped me with merciless force, spun me round and round and over and over . . . then under and down with my knees thumping against my chin and the salt water mixed with stirred-up swirling sand all finding its way into my nose and throat.

There I was, that Friday afternoon not long after school had let out, waiting for the Big Fellers and trying to pick the right one.

First came a series of uneven waves which I didn't attempt to catch. Then a tall fast-growing one loomed up about fifty yards away.

'Here comes a beaut!' shouted a bloke with a harsh voice.

Most of us decided to catch it. I waited a few seconds, then suddenly it seemed too close for a fair start. The others were already over-arming shorewards, so I copied them with a frenzy of strokes and that was the last I saw of them for the time being. I gulped air.

The Big Feller was with me now, lifting me up as it started to topple over right at its very peak. My arms stopped moving and I stretched them forward. My legs trailed behind limply.

Somehow I had managed to catch the wave, and though my eyes were open I tried to keep my head still because I knew that if it went back I would probably come up too fast and lose my wave.

So I didn't get another gulp of air until I scudded into shallow water then lost speed. Now I scrambled into a kneeling position and rested on my stiffened arms, getting my breath back and feeling proud of my ride—though it had all been a strain.

Was Sam watching? My eyes were sore, for I hadn't got used to the water yet, and the sunlight almost seemed to be attacking them. I couldn't pick him out in the muddle of sunbakers and kids on the beach.

Still sucking in air for all I was worth I turned back towards the deeper water.

This time I would try a ride with my arms alongside my body and my knees bent a little, the way Dad had shown me. I would maybe use my shoulders to try curving away from the breaking part of the wave, and so get a longer trip.

At first I was out of luck. A Big Feller caught me off balance, swung me all over the place like driftwood, then slammed me under. Ugh! A dumper!

That was no way to show Sam Rukovski how to body-surf. My eyes were stinging with salt and sand, like they usually did in early spring.

I didn't look towards the shore, but turned back for another go.

My body-surfing improved. I snatched ride after ride as fast as I could. My legs and arms began to ache. Sometimes it was a battle just to get a breath, but in the end there was no need for me to grit my teeth and I was even able to laugh.

I decided that the seventh ride was going to be my last. Perhaps it would be lucky seven.

Certainly that wave looked like the biggest Big Feller of the afternoon. It was so powerful that it knocked me right out of line. Whoosh! I shuddered right to my toe-nails!

But I fought my way back. I felt the blood in my head sing a happy song. I swished forward, forward, forward . . .

This time I didn't lose speed. With my head high above water level now, I spurted towards shallow water, and at last I scudded right on to the sand almost like a water-skier coming ashore. A beacher!

I lay there for half a minute, getting my breath back. The gentle little waves near the water's edge came lapping over me. I suppose I felt a surge of triumph when I stood up.

Sam was a short distance up the beach, crouching near one of the flags. His chin was resting on his knees. He pretended not to notice that I was back on the beach.

I stumbled over the warm sand towards him. 'Sam,' I panted, 'didn't you see? It's great, this body-surfing. Don't you even want to try?'

His eyes were closed. He was humming some silly little tune.

'Don't you want to try?' I insisted.

Sam came out of his huddled position like a spring uncoiling. Just flung himself at me.

I tumbled over backwards.

He didn't say a word, just pummelled me, thumping my shoulders and my stomach and my head. One blow stung my lower lip. Blood trickled from it.

Sam looked at the blood on his own fist. He stopped belting me and walked away up the beach towards the changing rooms on the Esplanade, with globules of sweat standing out on his head like raindrops in the sunlight.

I was left dazed—too dazed to yell any abuse after him.

Anyhow, what could I have said? 'Sam, you're a no-hoper for being so touchy.' Or: 'Sam, you don't have to learn to body-surf after all—you can live without it.' Or: 'Sam, I was a mean old dingo to flash my body-surfing around.'

As it happened, I had no chance to say anything.

Sam went up the steps to the Esplanade, not looking back. Soon he was out of sight, leaving me all alone on my beautiful beach, with no one to keep me company.

That's how hard things were for me, trying to be mates with Sam Rukovski.

So the only thing worth doing was to try a few stunts on my own. And I thought: Now if only I had that real surfboard. . . .

But I had to face up to the truth that a proper new board would cost more than a hundred dollars, and I didn't even have one dollar let alone a hundred. That big moment when I first obtained one seemed so agonisingly far away.

In the meantime I had to find something else to satisfy my craving for action in the surf.

TWO

SPEEDY FLASH

'Dad,' I said. 'A bloke needs some kind of thing to ride on when the waves are good.'

'Uh-huh,' he said, which didn't really tell me what kind of mood he was in.

'I've got to have something to ride on. Just a surfoplane.'

'Just a surfoplane,' he said in a hopeless voice.

'Gee, look,' I said, 'if you're near the end of sixth grade and almost set to go to high school and you don't have some kind of board, or at least a surfoplane, you're just about dead.'

A surfoplane may have been kidstuff in some ways. It was just an inflated mat of thick rubber up to about four feet long. But you could do things on it. More than on a flimsy skidboard, for instance, in only a few inches of water.

Dad took a gulp of his breakfast coffee. I ate a few of my rice bubbles and waited.

'Well then?' I said when he didn't answer.

'Some of your classmates don't seem to have surfoplanes, Greg. But they're not getting buried.'

'You know what I mean.'

He got up. At any time now he would be setting out for his job in the city.

'Dad, it's like that when you live at the beach,' I blackmailed. 'It's not much use living here unless you have something resembling a board.'

Mum was in the kitchen.

'You'd do better,' she called, 'if you did some thinking about all the bits and pieces you need for when you get to high school, after Christmas.'

Well, that was Mum's way of looking at things. I thought that it was probably because she came from Scotland that her mind always seemed to be on work and school.

'Aw, Mum,' I moaned. I was a duffer at school.

Dad went into the bathroom. He did some noisy tooth-cleaning. Then he finished his coffee and took his plastic lunch-box from the kitchen.

'How much does a surfoplane cost, anyway?' he said.

I bounced up and answered: 'Well, Dad, you can get one for as cheap as six, or maybe seven, or perhaps eight, or possibly nine dollars.'

'I see,' he said.

'After all, that's not like trying to have a real hot-dog board costing more than a hundred dollars, is it?'

'No,' he said, 'not quite.'

'Oh, Greg,' said Mum, 'you talk as if we're growing dollars instead of weeds in the back yard. And look at us, with an 8 per cent loan to pay on this old bomb of a house.'

Mum had the kindest blue eyes and the softest

pink cheeks you could imagine, but she looked as hard as a sheep-drover that morning. It had me scared, all this talk of the house-loan, for it was the thing that Mum used, to put the pressure on Dad. The house would probably fall down before we could finish paying for it, despite all the work we put in plugging up the cracks with cement and plaster.

'If you want a surfoplane, Greg,' said Dad before he left, 'then you damn well save up for one.'

That's how tough it was for me, trying to get my surfoplane.

It wasn't like that for all the kids around Bondi. Some people were making oceans of money. Some were just making a little. It was that kind of neighbourhood then, and it still is now.

For instance, in our grade at school there was a cove called Nick Hirst. He had about a dollar to spend every single day of the week. He could have a Coke or a hamburger or a spring roll or one of those Drumstick icecreams any time he wanted, before or after school. Most often he had the lot. He was as flabby as an outsize jellyfish.

Well, I remember once we were playing on the reserve with a mob of kids, just using a lump of rolled-up cloth for a ball. Then along came Nick.

'Hey, Nick,' shouted Jiranek, who had moved up to the high school already. 'Go get your Dad to buy you a football.'

'Yairs, go on,' said another kid, 'then you can play with us.'

'If you get one we'll make you captain,' said

Jiranek.

Off went Nick Hirst.

'And mind it's a League ball,' called somebody else.

Nick got the ball. We had our game. And all because his father was a slick businessman who made things easy for him.

It was never like that for most of us. I had 25 cents to spend every week, plus another 25 cents if I did some chores around the house and went to collect the groceries. That was about all that Mum and Dad could afford, and their own luxuries were next door to zero.

So even something like a surfoplane was not easy for me to come by.

'Why can't I start a paper run now, Mum?' I asked, messing about with my sausages and tomato sauce much more than usual.

'A paper run might be all right if you were starving, which is not so. Or for an older boy than you.'

'We are not exactly rich though, are we? And I am just about knocking on the high school door now, aren't I?'

'Paper runs are all right for parents who don't care where their children get to.'

This was not true, and Mum really knew it. The paper shop down on Campbell Parade had some lads from good homes on their books. But no, you simply could not argue with Mum when her neck went red from crossness and she was cleaning the room so vigorously that you might have thought it was deep in cow manure.

'I'll have to try and make a board then,' I said.

But I didn't know how to go about using resin, or poly stuff, or fibreglass to make a board. The surfies on the beach all seemed to have paid cash for theirs.

I spent all Friday evening trying to make some kind of skidboard out of the side of an old Bushell's tea chest. The wood went splintery all round and it never looked like becoming the right shape. Tea chests are fine for keeping pets in or for fooling around with in a rumpus room. They were no good for skidboards.

Maybe I could have made a belly-board out of the top of Mum's coffee table, but she couldn't seem to appreciate my needs. Just as well. It would have been a big joke on the beach.

Some of my friends would go down there and just borrow something. I hated borrowing. They used to have a ride or two on Nick Hirst's board, because he was too lazy to ride himself but brought it down to the beach to flash around.

I was too proud. When I went skimming about on the waves close to the shore it was going to be on my own piece of equipment, nobody else's.

One day I was going to surprise the boasters when I treated myself to that man-sized surfboard, smooth and slick and streamlined.

And no one would ride on that board but me.

How I was going to contrive to buy such a luxury I didn't know. Yet I was going to. Somehow.

In the meantime it had to be a surf mat.

'Mum,' I said, 'where's the *Sunday Telly*?'

'Greg, you talk like scrambled eggs,' she said.

'I'm talking about the ads in the Sunday paper. Free ads for us kids. Swaps and all that. I could put one in for this Sunday.'

'Oh, you're still going on about your surfoplane idea.'

I gave her a big smile. 'I can swap something then?'

'Not clothes. Or things you need for school.'

'My skateboard, and my collection of comic books.'

There was a big sigh from Mum. 'Well, I'd be glad to see those comic books out of the way. And your skateboard seems to make you fall a lot and get gravel rash—though you only had it new last Christmas.'

'I can't use it much now. Too many people on the concrete paths. And you wouldn't have to moan about the skin off my knees if I got rid of it.'

'I don't moan,' she said firmly. 'Anyway, how about that little board made of foam stuff?'

'Aw, that!' I puffed. 'I can't use that. It's kid stuff. Had it for years, and it's only about right for Clare now.'

This was true. Little Clare, all curls and freckles and still too young for school, used the board in the paddling pool at the north end of the bay. I wouldn't have been seen dead with a thing like that.

'Oh, well . . .' Lots of head-shaking from Mum. 'Go on.'

I grabbed a pencil and started to write out my

ad on a sheet of paper ripped out of an old exercise book.

It was the following Friday when I parted with my skateboard and comics. A boy from Centennial Park way did the swap with me. He was a good distance from the surf, and wanted to practise his balance and turning powers on the little springy board set on roller skates.

The surfoplane was a long way from being a real surfboard but it would keep me going. Fully inflated it seemed tough and well balanced. The kid I got it from had daubed on the name SPEEDY FLASH in red letters.

I hugged the surfoplane and ran down the grassy slope towards the beach. Down on the road near the surf club a big cream Holden came at me and almost mowed me down. The driver was a fat man. He had a red face and wore king-size sun glasses. He stood on the brake and thumped his horn, with the car curving over to the left and screeching like a dying pig and leaving black skid marks on the hot road.

The man didn't get out. He just used some foul language at me, then flicked the gear lever and accelerated up the slope towards the Junction.

I gulped and looked around to see if anyone had been watching. Hard to tell. The nearest person was an old man drinking a can of beer.

I took a deep breath, hugged my surfoplane tighter, then edged across the road.

'Kids . . .' said the old man with the can of beer. 'They ought to shoot the lot of 'em.'

Still it was good when I came to the bottom of the steps and felt the friendly beach beneath my feet. On the beach everyone was equal—me and the other kids and the driver of the big cream Holden.

The rubber of my thongs made squeaking noises on the scorching sand as I picked my way between the clusters of beach people and would-be surfies towards the flags. Ten thousand miles of wild ocean confronted me. Blue water and silver sand set my eyes adazzle and the breeze left its salt drying on my lips.

I did not see the kings of the surf as they chased the waves on their flashy fibreglass boards, for I was a sort of a king with the surfoplane and the beach belonged to me.

THREE

NET MAN, NET MAN, DON'T LET THE SHARKS GET ME FOR SUPPER

The waves were not too big that Friday afternoon, breaking gently from about three feet high. Just about as glassy as you ever saw them at Bondi.

Nick Hirst was down there near the flag at the south end of the beach. Jiranek, from the high school, was making use of Nick's board on the little waves close to the sand. Nick Hirst himself was too much weighted down by flesh to make the best use of it, and on the odd occasions when he flopped out on it he just about made it submerge. Funny thing was, his father occasionally made use of it and was far from hopeless.

When it came to swimming Nick wasn't bad. 'As slow as a Barrier Reef turtle,' said a beach inspector one day. 'But he can go just as far when he makes up his mind.'

Jiranek was clever on Hirst's board. He had a lean, wiry body, and although he had only been over here from Europe a few years he looked as much an Aussie as many a bloke whose ancestors came over with the First Fleet back in 1788.

'Hey, take a look at this,' he would screech when

31

he was making a little shore-break. And he would use his legs and body weight to guide the board on a twisting run around a wave crest, then make it curve back gracefully until it came to a stop almost at the water's edge.

'Hiya goin', Greg?' he called when I came near to where he was performing. 'I see you got yourself something to ride at last.'

'Yairs,' I said, 'just a little something to ride.'

'Want to know something?' He shook the salt water from his head as he talked in that boastful way of his. 'I shall be getting a real Shane surfboard, just for myself, when the Christmas hols come along. Hot dog, eh?'

I let the heavy rubber surfoplane rest against my thigh. 'Not a Shane, I'll bet.'

'All right, what will you bet?'

'A Shane?'

He moved a step nearer. The wet sand that stuck to his arms was shimmering in the sunlight. 'You heard, Stevens.'

'I heard, Jiranek.'

'Well?'

'You're just boasting,' I said, with jealousy hot inside me.

'If you come talking like that,' he said, 'you're going to get a dong round the ear.'

Jiranek was bigger than Sam Rukovski, and a lot stronger too. He was a different kind of animal though. Sam was a fanatic. Sam could overpower me just by sheer enthusiasm.

But Jiranek's strength was cancelled out because he was cautious. If it came to a scrap I could handle him, I felt sure. Being left-handed could be a help against him.

Still, I was down there on the beach to use my surfoplane, not to have a scrap. So I picked up the surfoplane and walked slowly down into the water.

My feet were scarcely wet when a handful of sand came zinging at me from behind, striking my left ear and the back of my neck. The shock of it made me stumble. I dropped my surfoplane.

My surfoplane, my precious surfoplane!

I bent down, fumbled for it, then turned round with anger sizzling up all over me.

Jiranek was just beyond the water's edge. He wasn't more than a dozen steps away. His arm was drawn back as if he was a baseball pitcher, and in his fist there was some more sand. The grin on his face made him seem ugly.

'You nasty-looking groper fish!' I shouted.

Jiranek made his throw.

I managed to duck the main ball of damp sand, although some of the stray bits went into my mouth and eyes.

I spat, blinked, then stumbled towards the shore. The third heap of sand missed me at close range as I dived at him. My shoulder went hard against his side, like a Rugby League player making a tackle. The shock impact brought instant pain to me, but at least Jiranek buckled and went down.

He was quick in recovering.

He brought his fist hard against the calf muscle in my right leg.

Gee, I thought, that hurt!

It made me so angry that I brought my hand down edgeways on his arm. He swung again, trying to grab my hair, but the barber had given me a short cut at Mum's request and Jiranek couldn't grab hold because the hairs were short and sweaty.

'I'll wipe the beach with you,' he threatened.

'Pigs might fly,' I said.

We had a punching session, partly on our feet and partly on the sand. The sand, some of it wet and the rest powder-dry, crept into our eyes, mouths, hair, and swim shorts.

It was a pretty warm day, about 88 degrees according to the 2UW weather man. There was sweat all over us. Sweat and sand.

Jiranek hit me on both eyes and on my teeth. I hit him on the nose and left ear. When I went down he rammed a foot in my stomach but I managed to put an arm-lock on his neck. Then we went almost motionless, just grunting like hogs and breathing hard.

Who would have won if the scrap had gone on was an evens bet. As it happened the beach inspector had the last say.

'Stow it, you two larrikins,' his voice boomed from almost above us.

The inspector was a tower of a man with a deep hairy chest and a hook nose. He wore a broad-brimmed white hat with the official badge on it. You couldn't argue with the badge, and you couldn't argue with the fierce look he directed at us.

But we wouldn't let go of each other. I was

scared to lose my grip in case Jiranek might dong me one. He was scared in the same way.

The inspector prodded us with his toe and snarled. 'Stow it, I told you!'

We let go together.

The anger stayed on the beach inspector's face. 'Let me find you causing a disturbance again, and I'll have you thrown off the beach. Understand?'

We understood. In a way, we must have been glad he had come. We puffed and spat out sand, then scrambled apart.

'Sorry,' said Jiranek to the beach inspector.

'Sorry, mister,' I said.

'You'd better be.' He glared at us one more time, then turned his attention to another group along the beach and wandered slowly away.

Jiranek scowled at me. I scowled back.

'Lucky for you he came, Jiranek,' I said. 'It saved you from getting licked.'

The bigger boy tightened up his fists again. 'You got a nerve, don't you, Greg Stevens? Just wait till you come up to the High. I'll get you there. I'll give you a working over behind the gym, you see.'

'Yairs,' I said, 'and pigs might fly.'

Having got back my breath by now I turned my back to him and splashed off into the water again. I half-expected him to be wild enough to defy the beach inspector and pelt me with sand again. But no sand arrived. Perhaps a sort of day of reckoning would come later.

It was terrible taking my first ride on that surfo-plane with Jiranek and Hirst looking on. You can't rush things too quickly on a surfoplane any more than you can on a hot-dogger's board.

For one thing, the air filling the four sections gives it a springiness which makes it difficult at first if you want to kneel up. You can't do things by numbers. You can't say: At the order one start paddling in time to catch the wave; at two kneel up and get balanced; at three try a curving run away from a breaking wave-crest.

Every wave is different, so you have to play it by ear. You have to be gentle sometimes, vigorous other times. You have to think of the surfoplane as a kind of projection of yourself.

At last I tried to catch a wave. The buoyant mat wouldn't help me, or the wave wouldn't.

Wipeout!

I tried again. Same result. A third time, a fourth, a fifth . . . more. The surfoplane acted like the devil with me the victim.

Following my scrap with Jiranek, all this tired me out. I felt like letting the surfoplane go drifting out to sea on its own. When I got started again I didn't really try, but strangely enough this was all I needed to do the trick.

I was riding. The mat moved so well that I could kneel up, and even catch my breath. My head was in the air.

The surfoplane raced towards the shallow water and I went down belly-flat again, paddling it to keep up the speed.

When it slowed down I turned it, without even glancing towards Jiranek or Hirst, and went back for more. It was strange how the tiredness had gone out of my mind as well as my muscles.

I rode in again.

And again.

Now I could hardly go wrong.

Suddenly it seemed that I was the King of Bondi, or maybe an albatross skimming the water, or a frogman finding a new green reef. I was a glider pilot, a ski-jumper, an astronaut, everything that had power, everything that felt joy.

The waves freshened, the surf grew. The sun sank lower over the land.

I didn't see Jiranek or Hirst leave the beach. I didn't see my father arrive. It was his voice that penetrated my water-drenched ears as I came close to the shore once again.

'Come out of it now, Greg,' he called.

I looked towards him, expecting to see anger on his face because I'd stayed away from home so late. But there was no anger, just an understanding smile and a hint of pride as he saw the way I'd fought myself out of trouble to master the bouncy surfoplane in the rough water.

The last of the swimmers and boardriders were heading shorewards. Dusk was coming fast and all the picnic people had drifted away towards home, leaving paper bags and lager cans and newspapers in the hollows where they had rested.

A draught of cool air blew in from the sea. Dusk, coming swiftly, brought its own curfew. Night was a time when only sharks and fools inhabited the surf.

I was glad I could find the strength to stand up, ready to walk home for something to eat. And I had to be glad about those net men who kept most of the sharks out of the bay. Who'd want to be a shark's supper?

I shivered at the thought of it, and walked away with Dad over the crinkly sand that was still warm from the heat of the day. We headed for the steps. My surfoplane was snug in my arms.

Mum gave us steak and chips that evening. I ate greedily just like a shark does at dusk, if it gets the chance. And like a shark I immediately began to think about my next victims.

But my victims were going to be waves!

FOUR

SO CLOSE TO THE BEACH BUT YOU CAN'T SEE THE SAND

Christmas Day hit Bondi like air coming out of a hot stove. There was the meanest apology of a breeze. You could wring the sweat out of your shirt, and oxygen was as hard to get as gas on the Birdsville track.

I took out my surfoplane, scanned the ocean, saw no flecks of white on the span of blue. Back went the surfoplane into the junk cupboard.

The three million people living in and around Sydney were being barbecued in a temperature reaching up to the century mark. People donned their lightest clothes, slide long cold drinks into their Esky boxes along with salad stuff and corned beef and sliced cheese and cans of tuna.

They jostled to the beaches. They descended on Dee Why and Manly, Cronulla and Maroubra, Coogee and Bronte. And, naturally, Bondi.

Bondi received more than its fair share. Bondi is the best known beach, and handy for the city. There were so many refugees from other suburbs that the locals couldn't find a piece of territory to call their own. The city people had left home early to find some place to park their cars or to pile on to the buses. Bondi people, except the surfing fanatics, were too casual. When they got down to the beach the whole area was in the hands of the enemy.

Christmas Day for us was a family affair. 'No, Greg, you don't go off on your own,' said Mum.

The house was quiet early on, despite all the traffic noises snarling at us to get up. We had breakfast then looked at our presents, or maybe we looked at our presents then had breakfast—I reckon that's more like it.

Clare was only four. A new kind of doll with blonde curly hair like her own sent her into a happy trance.

Being a lot older, I wanted something a bit more grown up, and naturally it had to be something for the beach. Dad saw that what little money there was available became well used. A snorkel tube and some flippers, I found.

Today I could get some excitement. Nothing like owning a real surfboard, but good fun for a fraction of the cost.

'Gee, Dad, that's great,' I said, letting him see me try the gadgets on a few times.

Mum packed up our picnic and we were all set to tramp off by ten thirty.

Where to go? Bondi was loaded up. We had no car.

'Tamarama,' said Dad.

'Fair enough,' I said. It's one thing you can do when Bondi reaches saturation point—go to Tamarama, the middie-sized beach just south of where we lived.

Tamarama is a good spot. It has real character, for families as well as surfies. There isn't much in the way of hotels, milk bars, delicatessens or filling stations—just steep slopes with springy grass, bold rocks and homes cut into the cliffs where banana trees and frangipani trees flourish in the sheltered air.

There's a surf club too, perched up high on the rugged cliff, and down below it the powdery sand with the long arm of the ocean reaching in with its blues and greens of every shade.

The Tamarama bay was heavily dotted with people, though nothing like as many as Bondi. 'We'll go down on the rocks round the point here,' Dad told us. The sweat was streaming down from his hair. 'You'll find lots of tide pools, and a couple of natural swimming holes. Clare can hunt prawns in the pools, and Greg can swim with me, and ...'

'And I can park myself in the shade of the cliff,' said Mum, breathing as hard as if it was laundry day.

Being away from my beach made me feel strange. I just never went away from my beach if I could help it nowadays, not when I had spare time.

We went back and found a spot. It was a good place, not too crowded and with nooks in among the rocks where we could change. I was in my swim-shorts in a few seconds. Dad was talking to a fisherman, Clare was ankle deep in a little tide pool and Mum was relaxing in the shade of a rock.

The water near the rocks was cool looking—

deep and green and clear and cool.

Though there had been no breakers worth calling breakers on the beach it was amazing how the sea moved around near these rocks. I dived in with my mask on, then got my snorkel to work. It was good to look down through the restless rays of light at the waving clumps of snoreweed and patches of pure sand between the slabs of stone.

Clare, who was not one to like the heat, had a great time in the tide pools where she was safe from the hazards of the ocean. Her collection of shells got larger and her freckles got frecklier.

Picnic time came and went. Mum read her *Australian Women's Weekly* then fell asleep in the shadows. Dad snoozed in the sun.

I dived and swam and snorkled until five o'clock when the shark alarm pierced the peaceful air. Everybody scuttled out of the water, with me heading the scramble. Dad shouted something to me and Mum stumbled towards me, demanding to know if I was all right.

The warning didn't last long, shark or no shark, and I was all for carrying on. Dad pointed to the sky. A dark curving bank of cloud grew even as we watched. The air was clammy, suddenly feeling cool. 'Let's go home,' said Mum.

On the way I had a view of my beach from the hill at South Bondi. The threat of rain had sent most people scampering for their cars and buses. Everything looked all right again, with lots of sand showing now and just a few surfies splashing about in the dark green water.

A breeze was starting to blow in from the sea. Soon there might be a bit of surf, however flat, and there would be a scurry to take out the idle boards to get a few short rides before dusk.

Now the first drops of rain fell and we took a short cut towards home, turning away from the beach front so that the ocean was behind my back.

'Enjoy yourself, Clare?' said Dad, picking up my sister and hoisting her on to his broad shoulders.

'It was fine, just fine,' Clare said in a happy, yawny voice.

He ran a hand through my salty hair. 'How about you, Greg?'

'Oh, great,' I said.

But I was thinking still about my Bondi Beach, and how I had really wasted a whole day of my life away from it.

Tomorrow I would be there again. Nothing was going to stop me.

FIVE

THE BEACH, THE BEACH, THE BEACH

The long holiday came, stretching right through January, and I always seemed to be surfing. Surfing or running down the beach on my way to surf. Every day after breakfast I was off and away the moment Mum said O.K.

Sometimes I was allowed to take my lunch down on the beach. Not always.

'The beach, the beach, the beach,' said Mum. 'It's all you talk about, all you think about. Always the beach. You're hardly through breakfast and away you rush as if the devil's after you. And supposing you don't come home for lunch, then I don't see you all that day, what with me working at the fruit shop in the morning and doing my chores around the house in the afternoon.'

'I always get my jobs done before I go, remember,' I said.

'Yes, you get your jobs done.' Mum started putting on her hat in front of the old oval mirror in the hallway. 'You get your jobs done so fast anyone would think the world was going to end if you didn't get down to the beach.'

44

'Aw, Mum.'

'That's all you can say. *Aw, Mum.*'

'Aw, I don't know about that, Mum.'

My mother looked baffled as if she was staring at a crossword puzzle that no one could solve. 'I can understand Clare, but not you . . .'

'Can I go, then?'

'All right, Greg, go on then. Have your lunch down there. Take some fruit, and get a meat pie at the Flying Pieman on the way down. Be back at five, though.'

'Thanks, Mum. Gee, thanks.'

'And don't forget to clean your teeth before you go.'

Fruit was cheap for us because of Mum's job. I took two nectarines, a banana, and three passion fruits.

Away I went—me, my surfoplane, my towel, and my fruit. The hot wind blew me all the way along the beach front to the pie shop.

Nobody ever made pies like the Flying Pieman. They were hot from the oven and all gooey with rich brown gravy. When you ate one you could feel the power grow in you. As I hurried to the green lawns across the road the pie seemed to be burning a hole in the palm of my hand.

The pastry was light and thin, the steak lean and tender. I would never be able to keep it in one piece until lunch time, and there was always the fruit . . .

So I sat on a bench facing the ocean and munched the pie, though breakfast was only an

45

hour and a half behind me.

The hot meat burned the tip of my tongue. The gravy flowed down my chin in a rich brown river. It was always like that when I had one of those pies. I peered towards Campbell Parade in case anyone was observing me with my sly snack, but there was no one I knew.

Soon the pie was gone. There was just me with my surfoplane, my towel, my fruit, and my feeling of guilt.

Ahead was the ocean, looking incredibly huge that day with its wave tops whipped into a frenzy by the wind. So I went off again, wiping my chin with my fingers then licking them clean.

And the beach welcomed me.

It was a different beach from the one people saw on public holidays. There were only a few grown-ups on holiday, a bunch of kids like myself, and that little band of surfboard kings who seemed to be free of the need for going to an office or factory.

Acres of unoccupied sand, thousands and thousands of gallons of unoccupied blue water, all for me!

The surf was ten feet tall that day. The waves were hollowed out, just to suit a hot-dog rider. I walked past the surfboard section of the beach and had to choke back my jealousy as I saw the sun-baked blokes all occupied so happily out in that bright watery world.

Sam was there, halfway along the beach.

His mother was with him. She wore dark glasses and was reading an *Australian Women's Weekly*.

He was digging at the sand with a large plastic spade, looking a lot younger than twelve. Australian boys don't spend their time digging in the sand when they're old enough to go to high school and the water is right for swimming.

I thought:

Sam, why can't you stop being a Polish Jew and go in the water like all the other Polish Jews are starting to do? Why, there's one of them who is a surf champ, Sam!

But I just said: 'Hi, Sam.'

And he said: 'Hi, Greg.'

He looked at my surfoplane, a bit enviously it seemed, and went on with his digging. Mrs Rukovski looked at me but said nothing.

'See you, then,' I told Sam.

'See you,' he said.

I went down to the water. He stayed in that spot all morning, digging furiously like a miner on the threshold of an opal seam. It seemed as if he wanted to show that there were other things in life apart from surfing.

My pie was sitting heavily on my stomach. I didn't swim yet. Squatting down on the sand I searched the bay with my eyes, something like a TV camera doing a panning shot. I started with the rocks around Ben Buckler point and ranged all the way across to the Pacific Hotel.

You could learn a lot just doing that, while the sun went on baking your body that was already cooked brown.

The body surfers, for instance. You watched the

way the good ones timed their approach when a Big Feller came rolling in. You watched what they did with their arms and their heads.

You ignored the few foam-board kids on the edge of the water. It was fun for them. They learned balance and timing. But you'd covered all that yourself.

You looked at the best of the coves on surfo-planes. Some of them were about as stylish as pigs on roller-skates. Others could do amazing shore-breaks and stunts that defied description.

And then there were the surfboard kings them-selves. You could watch them for hours. You could sort out the real stars from the phoney ones.

I forgot that there were other people around me until Jiranek came strolling my way. He was alone. He had no surfboard.

I felt like saying: 'Liar.' But I just said: 'Hi!' Not 'Hi, Jiranek' or even 'Hi, Pieface,' because that would have been too friendly.

Still, Jiranek wasn't too cocky that day and didn't seem as if he was going to start any trouble.

He said: 'Looking at the surfers?'

'The board-riders? Yes.'

'Just the good ones, I hope. Not those no hopers loafing around in a heap on the beach.'

I looked at the phoney surfers. They were lying about near the lifesaving reel. All kinds of expen-sive boards, well waxed but hardly used, were spread around them. These jokers seemed to spend most of the day rubbing sun oil on each other's backs.

'Look at their hair,' Jiranek said.

'I'm looking.'

'Bleached. Not by the sun or the surf. By bleach out of a bottle.'

'You're right, I reckon. They're a bunch of no hopers. A couple of quick flips not too far out where the surf has calmed down ... then that's their day.'

He nudged my arm, drawing my attention to someone way out in the big waves. 'Know who that bloke is?'

I saw the surfer cut right back up the hollow part of a wave, right up to the crest again. All the time he kept perfect balance, though he was well up to the front of the board getting every scrap of speed.

'He's great,' I said.

'He's a champ,' said Jiranek.

'I reckon I've seen him on the TV newsreel.'

'Reckon you must have, unless you've got sand in your eyes all the time. He went over big in Hawaii. They get waves more than 20 feet tall there, but he rode them.'

I rubbed my nose, thinking hard. 'He must have had a pot of money, being able to go all the way to Hawaii.'

'No, Greg. He had to be helped. People trusted him, and they got paid back. He works for a living.'

'Doing what?'

Jiranek fingered my surfoplane. 'Making surf-boards.'

All the breath came out of my body at once in

an unrestricted show of envy. 'What a terrific way to make a living.'

'But not just anybody can design hot-dog boards. You've got to know how to use them yourself, in every kind of surf.'

'You sure know about surf things, Jiranek,' I said.

I ought to have been hating him, but couldn't conceal my admiration.

'Quite a few things,' he said in a casual way.

'Where did you learn it?'

'Hanging about the real surfers and the lifesaving clubs, all the way from here to Wattamola.'

I chewed on my lip, then took a deep breath.

'Reckon I could do a bit of hanging around too?'

'Oh, sure. Stick around me and you'll learn plenty.'

'Sure?'

'Sure.'

I wondered about that surfboard he'd boasted about getting for Christmas. No sign of it yet. Was it just pie-in-the-sky talk?

Almost as if he read my mind and wanted to change the subject he pointed along the beach and said: 'Hey, take a look at that!'

'What?'

'Him.'

'Who?'

'Sam Rukovski!'

'Oh, Sam.'

'Look at him. Digging in the sand.' He chuckled juicily. 'Just digging a hole in the sand!'

'He looks happy, anyway,' I suggested.

'He going to be a big laugh up at the high school.'

'Forget him.'

'No,' said Jiranek, 'let's go and kid him along a bit.'

'His mother's there with him.'

'Ma Rukovski! What'd she do about it?'

'Come on,' I said uncomfortably, 'the surf looks great.'

'It won't go away.'

'Come on,' I offered, trying to get his mind away from Sam, 'and I'll let you use my surfoplane.'

'Oh, mate, why don't you knock it off? I'm going to get myself a real board, I tell you.'

'Not yet,' I said.

He thought about it. 'How about you? Are you chickening out because the surf is too big?'

I laughed. 'That'd be the day!'

'All right, so you're not scared. What then?'

'I'll body surf.'

'O.K.,' he said. 'I'm sick of riding that piece of foam, anyway. I'll body-surf too.'

'Good oh.'

'What are we waiting for?' he said with a grin. 'See if you can stay the distance alongside of me.'

I put my towel and lunch bag on top of the surfoplane and ran level with him to the water. 'Course I can stay the distance, Jiranek.'

I wasn't going to be outdone by Jiranek. The Slav accent was still thick in the way he talked, and I reckoned that no one except a dinkum Aussie

could teach me anything about body-surfing.

'Come on then, Stevens,' he whooped.

Well, my pie was just about digested. I burped once, maybe twice, then bent my knees and plunged forward as boldly as I could into the ocean.

SIX

'NEVER IN A YEAR OF SATURDAYS'

We were soon out there, chin-deep or more in the rise and fall of the ocean, waiting not too far from some older body surfers. Waiting for a Big Feller.

And we didn't have to wait long.

Before we were even properly set the daddy of all Big Fellers came biffing at us, sweeping us shorewards. I missed my stroke because I tried too late, and furthermore I missed taking the deep breath that Bernard Farrelly says you must have to stay buoyant. I just wasn't organised at all.

I fought the wave hard now, but it toppled me over. Over and under and down. Deep down, spinning like a shot-down plane. I fought for the top, where the light was.

At last I hit the air, coughing and spluttering. My eyes stung. My ears semed to swell up to the size of cabbages. Somehow I managed to sort myself out so that I was swimming smoothly again and facing the ocean.

Oh murder, I thought, Jiranek has left me for dead and he must have hit the beach by this time.

Why was I so scared? I didn't need to be, for out of my eye corner I glimpsed Jiranek not a couple of yards away. He had missed the wave too.

Allah, Allah, Allah be praised, I yelled, copying Dad when something went right just for once.

We both got the next wave, but badly. It took us only ten yards, no more.

'Beat you, Greg,' said Jiranek, but he swallowed water when he opened his mouth.

'Liar!' I screeched, and swallowed water too.

'I'll show you, then. Give it another go.'

'Too right.'

We fought our way out again. It meant that we had to crash our way under four big ones that had already broken, but we half-filled our lungs with air between each.

We got out to what we thought was the best pick-up spot. Jiranek trod water and waited. I copied him.

An extra big wave loomed up ahead of us, so far unbroken but soon to break.

'Now!' shouted Jiranek.

He turned. I copied.

We struck out together as if we wanted the wave not to catch us but knowing that it must catch us and that we were nothing without it.

The Big Feller was a monster that had voyaged from the very heart of the ocean five thousand miles away from shore. It had a brute force that scared me more than I had ever been scared before in my life. As it roared at me I imagined bulldozers, eight-wheeler trucks and express diesel trains coming screaming at me, backed up by bursting reservoirs, fighting bulls and giant forks of lightning.

I screamed for help, but mercifully the roar of the surf made the scream a whisper. The wave hoisted me up on to its crest and bustled me away.

It was so right, was this wave, and by a fluke my timing was so right that even if I had wanted I could not have let it duck me, all in a flung muddle.

I had to go with it. Just had to.

No white stallion with fluttering mane could have carried me as proudly as that wave did. No ski, surfboard, speedboat, hydrofoil, jet plane or interplanetary rocket could have given me such a feeling of speed, power, thrust and majesty.

My shoulders moved only a fraction of an inch now and then. My hands were flat against my thighs. My ears throbbed to the drumbeat of the surf. My heart sang the glad song of a victorious gladiator.

The ride seemed to last for an hour, a day, a week, or perhaps it was timeless.

It ended when the gallant wave conquered the beach, then went ripping back to cut through the army of waves behind it. It left me in a glad, limp heap in the shallowest of shallow water.

I looked to my right. There was Jiranek, lying belly flat on sand and water, panting in a kind of fury. He looked my way at almost the same moment.

He grinned.

Then I grinned.

He said: 'Wunderbar!'

I said: 'Marvelloso!'

'You'll never body surf like that again, Greg. No one could.'

'Never.'

'Never in a long summer holiday.'

'Never in a month of Sundays.'

'Never in a year of Saturdays.'

We gave it some thought. And then Jiranek said: 'We could try, though.'

'We could try,' I said.

Jiranek got up. So did I. He held out his hand, open in friendship. I held out mine the same way.

He gripped it. 'We're mates, I reckon.'

'Mates,' I said.

He punched me on the shoulder, but playfully. 'Buy you a Coke.'

'No need. There's lots of fruit in my lunch bag.'

'I'll still buy you a Coke.'

'All right, if you have some of my fruit.'

'A deal.'

We grinned again. It was a queer feeling, being mates with Jiranek.

Then I looked up the beach and saw that Sam Rukovski was watching us. His dark eyes had specks of light reflecting the sun.

He thumped a pile of sand with his spade, savagely.

SEVEN

IF IT DOESN'T TASTE HORRIBLE IT CAN'T BE GOOD FOR YOU

That wasn't the end of Sam's troubles on account of not being able to swim.

Second week of high school, Wednesday afternoon, a mob of us were taken for swimming at Nielsen's Park. Must have been nearly a hundred kids of different ages from eleven up.

When it was sport day you could choose cricket or tennis or judo or softball or swimming. I chose swimming. Imagine me choosing anything else.

Jiranek was now in his second year at the high. 'Judo for me,' he said.

'If you don't come swimming you're not my mate,' I said in a bit of sulk. The body-surfing afternoon seemed like a thousand years ago.

'That's up to you,' Jiranek said.

I didn't answer. I certainly didn't want to lose my mate, not when there was the beach for us at weekends. But Jiranek went off to judo and I stayed on the swimming list. It was the only school subject I was really good at!

Down at Nielsen's Park, on the south side of the Harbour, the swimming area was surrounded by a shark net. It was quite a beauty spot, with clean sand and trees and interesting rocks. There was a kiosk for drinks and eats, good changing rooms and showers and everything.

There were two buses to take us there, with three teachers in charge. The best one for swimming was Mr Gibbs.

Anyway, we were all getting off the buses outside the baths, with Mr Gibbs ushering us into position, when who should I see? It was my old mate Sam Rukovski, complete with a big purple towel rolled around a pair of striped swim shorts. He didn't say anything when I spoke. Maybe it was all the hub-bub round about us, or maybe he was pretending not to see and hear me.

What a sport for Sam to choose, in company with a hundred lively lads all waiting to make an al-mighty splash. My, how I pitied him. He was left like a lame duck as we bustled up the tunnel to the edge of the pool.

The word came at last from the teachers. 'All right, you can go in!'

We plunged forward like a mob of thirsty cattle at a water hole.

I struck out for one of the rafts swinging about in the middle of the pool. With no surf to hold me back it all seemed tame and simple. I was even level with some of the older boys in reaching the raft.

After clambering aboard I looked back to the water's edge. Out of the hundred swimmers only three were still lingering there. Two looked like weak newcomers from overseas. The other was Sam.

Poor Sam!

He was struggling about all over the place, thrashing like a fish in a net. His arms were flailing but his feet were still on the bottom.

He looked grotesque. I should have pitied the poor devil.

But I was just a fresh kid at high school, enjoying the best lesson of the week. There wasn't much time for pity. I stood up triumphantly and dived into the water. It was a clumsy dive, for I was short of practice. The only place for diving at Bondi is in the baths at the south end—and you have to pay to go in.

So I used most of the lesson to improve my diving.

If only Jiranek had been there. He would have made a game out of the diving and yet we would have improved just the same.

Mr Gibbs, a tall brown-faced man with hair as fair as mine, moved along the water's edge and started to coach the three non-swimmers. Soon it was Sam's turn.

'You there,' said Gibbs. 'What's your name?'

'Rukovski, sir.' Sam was shivering all over by now.

'Come on then, Rukovski. You'll be a good prospect for the Olympics if you put your mind to it.'

'Yes, sir . . .'

'Walk out further then face in here . . . Go on. No, further. Further . . . Now get your feet off the bottom and strike in for the shore.'

'Mr Gibbs, I . . .'

'Oh, come on. Make the effort, Rukovski. Swallow some water if you like. It's like medicine. If it doesn't taste horrible it can't be good for you!'

Poor, poor old Sam.

Two or three blokes on the raft were laughing at his efforts, but I could have cried for him.

'Forget it and we'll start again,' Mr Gibbs was pleading. 'Go on out. That's it. No, you're not going to drown in two feet of water. A big push off, boy. Come on, a great big push off. . . .'

So it went on, till it was time for all of us to get changed. Mr Gibbs got the other two non-swimmers starting to take a stroke or two.

But not Sam.

Poor Sam.

Later on that afternoon I saw him shrinking away into the darkest corner of the changing room. His skin was unusually pale. Almost grey. And he was shaking all over, just like pampas grass when there's a southerly buster blowing through a garden.

I said: 'Hi, Sam.'

He didn't answer.

It wasn't only because he felt miserable that he didn't answer. All the fretting and trying and struggling and failing had left him exhausted. He was so completely weak and lost that he was unable to speak a word.

Perhaps I could have done something to help Sam, like staying next to him and keeping him company on the bus.

But I didn't.

Somehow I felt that I didn't want him to be part of the world I was trying to live in. It was a world of dinky-dye Aussies. Beach boys. Surfers.

A world in which refugee non-swimmers didn't belong.

EIGHT

OLD ENOUGH FOR A PAPER RUN?

'Dad,' I said one day in February, 'I'm in the second year at the High now.'

'Second year at the High,' he repeated, sounding as if he had drifted into outer space.

'Yes, second year!'

'A ripe old age you are.'

'Old enough for me to be doing a paper run.'

He looked at me at last, from over the top of his trade union news-sheet. 'What in the name of Captain Starlight do you want to do a paper run for?'

'To earn money.'

He looked serious for once, snuggling his chin in his cupped left hand and resting his elbow on the corner of the armchair. 'I know we don't give you much cash to spend, Greg. But your mother doesn't want you doing a paper run, you know that.'

'You mean, I can't ever do one?'

'Maybe eventually . . . Oh, well, perhaps I mean never.'

I felt as if I was going shaky all over, so much was the fury that stirred up inside me. 'If that's the case, I'll never get a surfboard, will I?'

'I wouldn't say that.'

'Then what am I supposed to do to earn a bit of dough—become a pop singer or something?'

He tried to chuckle. It didn't sound so good. In a way he was on my side really, but he didn't want to sound disloyal to Mum. 'You seem to have some great rides on your surfoplane, Greg.'

How could I possibly explain to him? How could I convince him that although a surfoplane was all right at one time, things were different now I was older?

'Dad, Dad,' I said, 'can't you understand that it's a real brand new, mansize surfboard I need? A McCoy, or a Farrelly, or a Shane, or a Platt. Look, Dad, I'm well over five feet tall now. I'm big enough to ride out there with the real surfers. I can swim like a dolphin and paddle like a Red Indian. Mum needn't be scared any more.'

'Nothing,' he murmured. He sounded as if he was at the other end of the ocean. 'Nothing except outsize waves, and sudden rips, and underwater rocks in surfing runs at places like Tamarama. And cramp. And sharks.'

'Aw, Dad, Dad. . . .'

He took a very deep breath. It seemed to reach right down below his belt and stay there for a while.

I waited for him.

It was a long time before he said anything further.

Then at last he said: 'Well, Greg, I suppose if your heart is burning away for want of the real surfboard, and we can't buy one for you, we'll have to let you do somehing about it.'

That was all he said to me about it. But it was enough. The powerful wave of my enthusiasm and determination had finally crashed through all opposition and had hit the shore.

It was a day to remember for ever. It was the day Dad took up my cause, the day he had the biggest of all arguments with Mum since the buying of the house near the beach. The day he won. . . .

I looked at the clock. Five minutes to seven, and the sun very low over Bellevue hill. The paper shop would be closing any time now.

I hunted for my thongs, couldn't find them, so I ran barefoot out of the house calling, 'Gee, thanks, Dad.'

Off I went along our dusty road towards Hall Street; past the post office and the delicatessen's and the milk bar to the warm bustle of Campbell Parade, where I dodged my way through loitering teenagers and fast-walking older people until I came to the entrance of the paper shop.

Unbelievably, the door was not closed!

NINE

WAITING IS WORSE THAN WIPE-OUT

Days passed.

Weeks. Months. It's seemed almost like years.

I worked. Worked and saved. Every morning at six o'clock I was awake and about, rain or shine, then after a drink of milk and a snack like a fried egg sandwich I set out from the newsagents with the papers.

How good the work was depended on the weather and the day of the week. In July when the keen winds blew from the Antarctic wastelands it was tough pushing the heavy bike around or towing the old pram. If there was a sudden darkening of the sky and the heavy raindrops began to beat down on me it was tougher still.

On Wednesdays and Saturdays it was hard work because the *Herald*s and *Telegraph*s were loaded with adverts on those days and so the papers were much heavier. Then I felt like throwing the job up and giving away the whole idea of saving for the surfboard. This was a big temptation in the winter when the windswept beach was empty except for a couple of fossickers near the water's edge, and a

bunch of husky blokes practising Rugby League, and a solitary tough surfer in a wet-suit.

But I kept going somehow.

The people in the paper shop were a great help. They didn't snap and snarl if I made a couple of mistakes like giving somebody a *Telegraph* instead of a *Herald*, or *Pix* instead of an *Australian Women's Weekly*. And once in a while they'd give all their newsboys a treat like a free feed and a trip to the theatre and you felt that life was good and that what you were doing was worth while.

Some of their old newsboys had really got on in the world. One was a journalist. Another was a sports star. Maybe we all looked a bit like no-hopers when we wandered the streets in the earlier hours, dressed in our scruffiest clothes, but in some ways it was like belonging to an exclusive club.

So I kept going while winter lingered on, then reluctantly gave way to spring, bright and warm and happy-feeling.

Spring seemed to be with us for a long time, which was a good thing because I wanted that board before summer came with its seven-week holidays and the promise of day after day of surfboard riding in the off-shore breezes.

Every Friday when my paper run was over I'd call at the shop and collect my wage. I suppose it wasn't a lot but it seemed a lot and I rarely spent any of it.

As soon as the Commonwealth Bank opened I was there ready to hand the money over the counter with my crumpled grey passbook, and a comforting

68

glow spread through me as I saw the number of dollars increasing week by week. I kept my book in an old powdered-milk tin under the bed and every night at bedtime I would take it out and examine it carefully to see that everything was all right.

One thing I promised Mum. 'When I've got enough dollars for the board, Mum,' I said, 'I'm not going to quit the paper run. I'm going to keep on with it for a while so that I can pay some cash into the family budget. I reckon we could do with it.'

'I reckon,' said Clare, eavesdropping.

'We'll see,' said Mum.

Then there was a Friday when I came back to the shop after my paper run and all the waiting was over. I smiled a special big smile when they handed me my week's pay.

At last I had enough for the bargain board advertised by a Brisbane firm in one of the surfing papers. A new board that no one else had ridden!

I went home like a whoosh.

Dad was there, lost in the sports pages of the *Herald*. I jostled him out of it. Then minutes later we were at the counter of the Commonwealth Bank in Hall Street.

'Well, well!' said Dad when my fists were full of dollars. 'You'll need someone to ride shotgun with you wherever you go.'

'Nobody needs to ride shotgun,' I said. 'I won't have this stuff long enough.'

No doubt I could have sent the money straight through the bank without even seeing it. But I wanted to see it before it went. I wanted to handle it myself. So I took it all to the post office down the street and got Dad to help me send a money order for 84 dollars to the Brisbane firm, complete with a form I had filled in about my weight and height and everything.

'There,' I said when everything was fixed up, '84 dollars for a board worth 120 dollars.'

We emerged from the cool of the post office into the bright sunlight. 'Let's hope everything will be O.K.,' said Dad.

'It will be O.K.,' I said. But secretly I was worried sick. My money could get lost in Brisbane, or maybe my board could get damaged in the freight. Or stolen.

It was a nail-biting time for me, waiting for my board. I'd sworn that I wouldn't go near the beach until it arrived and I could take a ride in style. But when an off-shore breeze sprang up I found myself wandering down to the edge of the sand and looking at the breakers and picturing myself battling out through them then rip-roaring my way back towards the shore. . . .

What could I do with myself? I couldn't just stand there and watch the surfies twisting and turning on their boards, because envy brought warm tears to my eyes. I was even jealous of their wipe-outs, because I knew that I was going to have a good many failures and that they were all part of the exciting journey towards success.

I crept off home. Dad was at work in the dock-yard now and Mum was quietly going about her chores, while Clare was organising her dolls into an endless series of games that made her oblivious of the real world around her.

For once I offered to do chores in the house. My mother looked at me as if I had become the victim of some aboriginal magic, but set me to work with some liquid floor polish. This I spilt on the carpet. Then I was asked to wash the dishes, and I broke a soup plate.

Finally, in utter despair, my mother sent me to the milk bar for a carton of cream. I managed to carry it home safely, but it looked as if there were no chores left that Mum would trust me with. On this occasion she merely wanted me out of the way for a little while.

I was tempted to grab the surfoplane, now scarred from old age, and try a few runs on it. The trouble was, I had been boasting in front of Jiranek and Hirst. 'The next time you see me in the surf,' I had told them, 'I'll be on a real gas surfboard, fit to ride any wave from Malibu to the Bower, with a redwood stringer down the middle and a tough streamlined skeg, a golden board. . . .'

'Golden board!' snorted Hirst. 'You just have to be kidding.'

Later, I couldn't think what had got into my mind to say *golden board*. It was just sheer bragging, nothing else.

Now I didn't dare to show my face around the beach until I could march down there with a real surfboard balanced on top of my head. As for it being golden, the only thing I could think of doing was to go to the shop and spend a little of what money I had left on a pressure pack loaded with gold paint. This I did. When the board came—if the board came—I would spray some gold along the rails to make them gleam in the sunlight.

That would make Nick Hirst give his big mouth a rest, I told myself.

But when morning came and the light began to sneak into my room I was already half-awake, worrying about the surfboard. It was quite a relief to get out of bed. My paper-run no longer seemed to have much meaning, yet I was glad to be doing it because the weight of the *Herald*s and *Telegraph*s took my mind off the king-size package I was dreaming about.

Three more days crawled past. Still I kept clear of the beach. Then a letter came. It said my order was being attended to. Well, that was something.

More waiting.

All those months while I had been saving up my newspaper money I hadn't reckoned on anything like this. I had simply pictured myself sending off the order then, almost by return, receiving a pop-out surfboard that hadn't even got the fingermarks of another surfer on its shiny surface.

But now, all this waiting.

Oh, the waiting, the waiting—it seemed like a kind of torture when all I craved for was action. Worse than a wipe-out, it was.

TEN

UP AT SAM'S PLACE

Saturday came round again, but still the board didn't.

'Mum,' I said when it was mid-morning, 'are you sure the board didn't arrive during the week while you were down at the fruit shop? Are you sure they didn't call with it and go away?'

She handed me a glass of chocolate milk, all frothy on top from the whisking when the powder was mixed in. 'Stop worrying, Greg,' she said with a smile that was full of kindness. 'If there was anybody calling with a monster package like a surfboard then the people at the garage would have seen them and taken it in for us.'

'Maybe I'd better ask them . . .'

'I did already. Every day.'

'Nothing?'

'Nothing.'

'Caw!'

I drank my chocolate milk and it made me feel stronger. Then I got hold of a sheet of notepaper and a biro, and I composed a letter to the surf firm.

It said:

Ten days ago I sent you a money order for 84 dollars. It was for a bargain surfboard. You haven't sent the board yet. Please send the money by return.

It was a milder letter than the one I had composed in my mind beforehand, for in that imaginary outburst I had demanded by money back. It had occurred to me that I might be able to get a second-hand board at a surf-shop or through the ads in the *Telegraph*, but after I had taken a few deep breaths I decided the brand-new board was what I wanted and that nothing else would do.

I managed to post the letter without having it censored by Mum. If Mum had seen it she would have made me word it even more politely, probably cutting out the words 'by return'. Scottish people are brisk and forthright but it was part of her character that she was always gentle with strangers.

The soft plunk of the letter falling into the mail box gave me some satisfaction, though it annoyed me to think that it just had to wait there until somebody from the postal service took the trouble to collect it. Then there would be a delay during sorting, and time on the Brisbane plane, and a delay until the letter was opened in the office, and time while they did something about it.

Oh, the waiting . . .

I was looking gloomy when Sam Rukovski came breezing down Hall Street in the direction of the beachfront. Nobody ever saw him looking so pleased with himself. There was colour in his cheeks for once, and the way he walked, it was almost like skipping along.

'Hi, Greg!' he said in a perky voice.

'Hi,' I said without enthusiasm.

'You don't look so good, Greg? What's up? Are you sick or something?'

'I'm fine.'

'You don't look fine.'

Heck, I wasn't going to admit that I was looking dismal because of waiting for my surfboard. 'I can't help the way I look, Sam.'

There was a big grin from Sam. 'Look, I'll buy you a Coke, Greg. All right?'

'I'm not thirsty,' I said. It was a lie. I was very thirsty. And short of cash.

'Come on,' he said.

'All right.' Even if there was reluctance in my voice, I was relieved that he had bothered to persuade me. I had started to hand over my paper-run earnings to Mum now.

Sam strutted off into the milk bar with me following, a bit like a hanger-on going after a benefactor into a pub.

The Coke was comforting. I drank the can so dry that there were rude noises when I sucked on the straw to get the last drops. Sam smiled more than ever.

'You're looking pleased with yourself today,' I said. 'What's happened in your life that's so marvellous?'

75

'I'll show you,' he said.

'Show me?'

'Sure thing.' His face was glowing like a Port Kembla blast furnace at midnight. 'Come on home with me and I'll let you see.'

'Aw, I dunno.'

'Come on.'

'All right,' I said.

I just couldn't get over the change that had come over Sam. Usually he was so jumpy and grumpy, seeming to want friends yet not wanting to become part of the action. Now you'd have thought he was a champ at something, with me the duffer.

We walked three and a half blocks from the milk bar, with me puzzling all the time about this mysterious something-or-other that Sam was going to reveal to me.

The Rukovskis lived in a smart home unit in a newish block in the direction of Bellevue Hill. Their unit was at ground level. Behind it was a back yard with a row of six garages. They owned the end one.

Sam said in a sort of electronic voice: 'Take a look at this.'

I looked. He gripped the handle of the swing-up door with his scrawny fingers and sent it rumbling upwards. There was no car inside. I could see the mysterious something-or-other immediately.

During our stroll through the streets I had been thinking of a few possibilities. Like a pair of roller skates ... a go-cart ... a surf-skate for a dry-land surfie ... a movie projector, even.

I was wrong with all these guesses. It was just a bike.

Just a bike. But man, what a bike!

It was only the flashiest bike that ever was assembled—the very latest lightweight model, all shiny chrome and crimson and gold. You never saw such a bike.

Sam grinned like the king of the world. 'What do you think?'

My tongue moved, but no words came.

I was flabbergasted because Sam's people, though better off than mine, were not the kind to sling their money round on luxuries.

'What do you think?' he persisted.

'Not bad,' I said.

'Not bad!' he screeched. 'You're just the maddest.'

'All right, Sam, it's fine,' I said, 'just fine.'

I ran my hands over it in the most casual way I could manage, testing the horn and brakes and multi-speed system and everything.

'Bet you wish you could ride it,' suggested Sam.

'You mean, I can try it out?' I murmured.

His face screwed up in horror. 'That's not allowed. Nobody else but me can use it. Dad says so.'

I pulled a sick face, and let him take hold of his bike. He fondled it as though it was a pet cat.

'That's that, then,' I said. 'Can't think why you bothered to bring me up here.'

'You could watch me ride it.'

'That's a laugh. You know me, Sam. I do things,

not watch others.'

He winced, remembering the way he opted out on swimming. 'There's my old machine over here ...' He nodded towards a dusty bike in the corner. 'You can ride that, maybe, if you can keep up with me.'

I made a snorting noise. 'Keep up with you! I could leave you for dead!'

'Like to bet?'

'Nuts.'

'Try it, then.'

'On that old bomb?'

'If you're so good.'

'I'm not so good. But good enough.'

He leaned his new treasure against the wall. He pushed the duty black machine towards me. 'There you are.'

I cocked my leg over and tried the saddle for size. The pedals were well within reach because Sam was an inch or two smaller than I was.

'Where do we go?' I asked.

Sam perked up. His black eyes were shining. 'There's a good run I'll show you. We zig-zag up the side streets towards Bellevue Hill, then whiz down again, pell mell. It's a great course.'

'All right,' I agreed. 'I'll follow you to the top, then when we come down the slope I'll wait for you when I get to the bottom.'

'You haven't got Buckley's chance,' Sam told me. 'It's going to be the other way round, man. I'll be right here waiting for you.'

'We'll see about that.'

I followed him up the dusty streets, some of them stinking hot in the midday sun, others with a welcome coolness in the shade of tenement buildings. By the time we reached the top my T-shirt was soaked with sweat and I was puffing so hard that I shook all over.

Sam, on the other hand, looked almost cool. He smiled at me in a sorry-if-I-made-it-tough-for-you way. His eyes glowed like two bright moons.

I had never seen Sam look so confident as he did just then. His confidence needled me like a thousand bindi-eyes.

Right, Sam, I said under my breath, *I'll get my revenge on the downhill run.*

ELEVEN

GOING DOWNHILL FAST

'Shall we get going now?' Sam said.

'If you like,' I answered in a casual way.

'Make it a race?'

'If you like.'

'Come on then,' he said, as eager as ever, 'let's go.'

'No, wait.'

'What's up? You chickening out?'

I fidgeted with the front wheel. 'This tyre ... It's soft.'

He dug his thumb down into it. 'Pump it up then.'

'Give me your pump a minute,' I said. There wasn't any pump on the old bike.

He thrust the pump into my hands and watched me work at the tyre. I could have done without all the pumping while we were resting at the top of the hill, but I suppose I'd asked for it.

I handed back the golden-plated pump then ran my arm across my forehead. I looked at my arm. It was soaking with sweat. I put my tongue-tip against it and tasted salt. I wished I'd put more salt on my eggs that breakfast time, because Mr Gibbs up at the high school had told me that you need salt in you to make up for what you lose in perspiration and the Olympic athletes take salt tablets. I wished I had some.

I wished I wasn't up there on top of the hill, waiting to race down. Why wasn't I in the surf?

Sam looked as if there was nowhere else he would rather be. He let a truck go past then said: 'Right.'

Away we went down the swinging road, dodging the occasional pit in the asphalt and pulling close to the side when a taxi came buzzing us. Sam was soon into the lead by two or three yards but I reckoned I could make up this distance on some of the toughest bends.

Yet when the first real bend came and we were safely round it Sam was still ahead. It was strange because he seemed to have stopped pedalling befor I had when we'd hit the curve.

All the same it felt good on the straight part that followed. Our downhill momentum was so powerful that it felt as if a cool wind was blowing in my face. Hair that had irritated my eyes on the big uphill climb was now blowing back and the sweat was already dry on my skin.

Another bend. Sam seemed to lose his pedalling rhythm as we came out of it and the old bike swung forward bringing my front wheel close to the white plastic tail flap at the rear of his new bike.

He edged forward a bit then I put in a sprint and stayed with him till the final bend. A lot of thoughts flooded my mind. Sam ought to win really. It meant so much to him. I had surfing but he only had the bike-riding.

Yet it wasn't in my nature to let someone beat me. In a race where there was only a first and second, with no third or fourth or back marker, I didn't want to be the one who came second.

Sam tried to settle things. Coming out of that final bend he produced a magnificent burst and pulled away to ten yards ahead.

'He's won,' I moaned.

Now came the worst part. We had to cross the South Head Road and drift off right towards Sam's place. There was plenty of traffic around as usual.

Sam pulled out into the middle of the road, shot a look over his shoulder at me and the following cars, saw the way clear, and swerved sharply over. He was in the side turning and out of sight by the time I was in a position to follow him off the main road.

'Yes,' I moaned, 'he's won.'

But in the side street, empty of traffic and only a few gasps away from the journey's end, disaster hit Sam. There was loose gravel outside a driveway. Not properly out of its curve, Sam's bike encountered the gravel and went into a violent skid. Seconds later he was on the road and almost under my front wheel.

I went all panicky. 'Look out!' I screeched.

I braked. Not the back brake on its own. Not even both brakes together. I didn't know which was which.

Just the front brake, that's all I pressed.

I skidded too. The old bike I was riding went all of a twizzle and pitched me over the handlebars, right on top of Sam and his beautiful new bike. The old bike spun on for a few more yards and came to a stop, then all was silent except for gasps and grunts and groans.

Sam spoke first when I crawled off him. 'You clumsy fat wombat!' he snarled. 'You wrecked everything.'

Rage gripped me. 'Clumsy your lousy foot,' I said. 'You brought me off.'

He scrambled to his feet and pulled his precious bike on to the footpath. 'I was winning,' he said. 'I was winning.'

'It's a draw,' I told him. 'At least you didn't lose.'

'I was winning . . .' He was trembling from head to toe as he dusted down his machine then straddled it to put the handlebars back into line. 'It's been scratched. I'll get hell from Dad.'

'It's all right, Sam, honest it is. And the old bike's O.K. too. Not a mark on it.'

I pushed it towards him to let him see that there was nothing wrong with it.

'I don't mind about that thing. It's my new bike, you idiot. It cost ninety dollars, all of that. I'll get hell . . .'

The skin was right off both my knees and there were tiny pieces of gravel sticking in the red raw parts. My right hand was grazed all around the knuckles too and it stung worse than the knees.

'At least,' I reminded him, 'you didn't end up under a bus.'

'I was winning,' he said, ever so faintly.

'What does it matter? It was only a bike ride . . .'

'Winning . . .'

'Come on,' I said, 'let's push the bikes the rest of the way. Not far to go.'

I thought he was never going to move from the spot where he stood caressing the marvellous bike, but the driver of a cab gave us a frightening honk because we were obstructing a bit of the street and Sam limped away after me.

He didn't speak any more on the way back so I didn't either.

But when the bikes were finally stowed away in the Rukovskis' garage and I gave him a wave as I walked off towards home he was still muttering something about winning.

When I arrived home the house felt strange. Mum and Clare were home, but not Dad.

'Where's Dad?' I asked.

'Gone,' said Mum.

I chewed at my lip and waited for her to say more. Something like: 'Gone to post a letter' or 'Gone to buy some shaving cream' or even 'Gone to look at the ocean.'

But Mum didn't add anything else. There was just the 'Gone' and that was all.

I moved closer to her and saw that her eyes were red. 'Gone *where*?' I asked.

'To Cooma. He's got a job in the Snowy Mountains . . . His mate, Jack Newport, called an hour

85

ago offering him a lift if he got a move on. They reckon there's still big money to be made in those parts, and Dad thinks it'll solve our problems about the mortgage.'

The shock of Dad not even waiting to say goodbye was bad enough. Now the talk of mortgage problems had me feeling almost ill.

Clare, sitting at the kitchen table, started sobbing. Mum was standing awkwardly, running her hands through her hair.

'You had a bust-up, didn't you?' I suggested in a bit of a hardish voice. 'About money, I reckon.'

'We had a bust-up, yes,' agreed Mum. 'We're badly behind with the payments on this house, what with all the money we've had to spend on repairs. And then your Dad was given this offer.'

I suppose it was unfair of me to look on Dad as a deserter then. His sudden departure had been courageous really, and goodbyes would have been awful for everybody. Probably it was realistic, too, for lots of people had been making big money just on labouring work in the Snowy, provided they kept away from the gambling rings.

But all this didn't stop me feeling bitter. As far as I was concerned Dad had freaked out, and I told Mum this in the bluntest terms.

My outburst only made Clare blub harder, and Mum look angrier.

What with the trouble as well as the flare-up over Sam's bike, it had been just about one of the rottenest days I could ever remember.

TWELVE

'YOU'LL JUST HAVE TO WAIT'

During the next few days I seemed to have Dad on my conscience all the time. It was the end of the school year. Holidays were due. Seven weeks of warm weather. All I had to worry about was wondering if my surfboard would come.

Perhaps if I had put my surfboard cash into the family budget in the first place, Dad would have been encouraged to stay at home instead of slogging his guts out at the Snowy.

Sam was on my mind, too.

Sure, it had been his idea to go up to the top of the hill, his idea for it to be a race down again. And he had been the one to skid first. At the same time, the thought of Sam failing to achieve what he had set his heart on troubled me.

At school I avoided being anywhere near him. This was fairly easy because he was in a different class and the school was big. Somehow I felt that if I came face to face with him I wouldn't be able to look him in the eye. Yet there was no explanation for this. I had done nothing to be ashamed of, only tried my darndest to win.

Perhaps in my heart I knew that by the pressure I'd put on Sam in that downhill race I had made him try to go quicker and quicker until disaster came.

Oh, heck . . .

Why didn't the surfboard come?

It didn't come. The last day of term was with us, and still no surfboard. Jiranek came breezing up to me when I was buying a hot pie at the tuckshop that lunchtime. 'What about your great surfboard?' he said. 'That wonderful golden surfboard!'

'It's on the way,' I growled.

'So is Christmas,' he said with the biggest grin of the year on his face.

'What's it to you?' I said.

'What bit you, Greg?' he mocked. 'Was that wonderful golden surfboard just a big dream, or what?'

I licked away a bit of tomato sauce that was dripping off the edge of my pie and used this as an excuse for not talking. Then I started to edge away towards the playground.

'Just a big dream . . .' His voice chased after me.

I turned back towards him and answered so violently that I spat out crumbs. 'It wasn't a dream, Jiranek, and if you want your teeth pushing down your throat you're asking for it.'

A prefect stepped forward and ushered me out to the bright sunlight, threatening a million detentions if I didn't behave myself in the tuckshop zone. I didn't talk back at him, but I glanced over my

shoulder and saw Jiranek standing there grinning
... grinning ... grinning ...

But I knew it wouldn't do any good even if I
waited for Jiranek after school, even if I excelled
myself and got the better of him, even if I broke
his teeth. There was going to be only one thing to
silence him properly—the sight of me with that
super surfboard itself.

And for the present I had no surfboard. Nothing
to make a golden flash against the Pacific blue.

Nothing for me again when I reached home. No,
said Mum, there was no mistake. No one had called.
'You'll just have to wait,' she said. 'I've enough to
think of, with Dad away.'

Evening came, and oh how it dragged. I couldn't
bear to look at the waves, and the occasional sound
of the surf thumping on the shore infuriated me.

At bedtime I got out a pile of my old western
and space comics and read them for hours by the
yellow light in my dank bedroom. Mum put the
light out at eleven, angrily telling me I would
'Wreck my eyesight'. Certainly my eyeballs felt
as if they were on fire.

Eventually I rummaged among my odds and
ends and discovered an old flashlight. The battery
was run down but there was just enough of a glow
for me to carry on reading till eventually the tiny
globe had only what looked like a spark left.

So I slept.

When morning came and Mum called me I
didn't want to get up. It was the first day of the
holidays. I had thought this was going to be the

best holiday of my life, but what could it be like if I didn't have my surfboard?

I clung to my bed. It took three calls to get me out, with no Dad there to grab me by the big toe.

By the time I arrived at the newsagents I was half an hour behind time. I struggled with a loaded barrow on Campbell Parade, thinking how when my paper run was over I'd go to the post office and phone the surfboard firm, long distance to Brisbane itself, and tell them a few things.

Then of all people, who should come walking along Campbell Parade, carrying a brand-new surfboard!

Jiranek!

There he was, strutting along—fortunately on the other side of the road—only about fifty yards away from me. His face had an engulfing smile, for the board balanced on his head was a sleek Shane, by the look of it, and that was the board he had once boasted about.

If he should see me now! Oh, how he would brag about his new surfboard. And how he would jeer because I hadn't the one I'd been telling everyone about!

I stumbled into the nearest doorway. Fortunately it belonged to a barber shop that was not yet open. I squatted down behind the yellow barrow that held the papers. With a bit of luck Jiranek would be so puffing out his chest and bracing the biceps that held the board in position that he would pass without seeing me.

A woman in a blue plastic raincoat looked down

at me in passing. The way she stared, I could have been some no-hoper drongo from the Cross. *Go on, buzz off*, I thought—*you and your glued-on eyelashes.*

The woman went on her way, but the worst thing was that there was now no one between me and Jiranek. I could only just squat there and hope he wouldn't see me.

Then Jiranek, as if by instinct, started to turn in my direction. *Heck!*

As his head moved, a puff of breeze lifted the board slightly and almost made him lose control of it. He was so busy getting a proper grip and edging out of the way of a husky-looking man that he did not turn in the direction of the barber shop again.

Half a minute later he was strutting down over the grassy bank towards the beach.

I came out of my foxhole, embarrassed because two other passers-by had noticed me huddling there with my newspapers.

The paper run was a drudge that morning. I threw the *Herald*s and *Tele*s with extra force into doorways and worked myself into a volcanic fury against all surfboard makers and all boys like Jiranek who had their own boards . . . and a Dad around the house.

When I arrived home, Mum was out shopping and Clare was still fast asleep.

I was hungry. Mum would probably be bringing something good for breakfast but I didn't want to wait. I spread two slices of bread with thick butter,

then spread tomato sauce all over the top of that.

With this feast going down I thumbed through the pages of our own newspaper, looking first at the funnies then at the sport and then at other snippits. A bit about Bondi hit me right in the peepers. It was all about surfboards—how a thief had been stealing some when surfies left them for a few minutes.

That was a lousy thing to do. Usually people could leave their boards around all day and not have to worry about them disappearing. This was a new threat. To me it was a crime as bad as horse-stealing in the days of the Wild West.

They'd better not touch my board, when I got it. I found myself thinking up suitable tortures for anyone who dared to even think of the idea.

Now I started to get even more worried. Supposing the package had already been sent from Brisbane and the surfboard thief had managed to grab hold of it if the delivery people had left it outside the door.

I felt sick at the thought.

After grabbing some coins I dashed out of the house, all set to make that call to the surfboard firm.

I slammed the door behind me, so hard that a flurry of plaster came tumbling down from the woodwork. I flip-flopped angrily down the few yards to the gate, vaulted over it then set off down the cool side of the street.

If I had been a minute earlier I would have

missed seeing the big delivery truck which skidded into our street then shuddered to a halt right outside our house.

Yes, *our* house.

THIRTEEN

LUCKY FOR SOME

Minutes later there was an enormous package in the lounge-room.

It was my board at last. I knew it was my board.

I struggled with the wrappings. Soon there was paper and string and padding all over the place, and then at last I had the surfboard balanced on the table.

If only Dad was here to see . . .

There was smooth, shiny yellow on most of it, and a white zig-zag pattern. Everything seemed to glint as sunlight streamed in through the window. I ran my fingers over the surface. I felt the balance of it, gloated over the design.

Mum came in, loaded up with the groceries.

'Mum,' I gloated, 'I've got my board at last.'

'So I noticed,' she said, wading all through the mess.

'I knew it would come,' I said with the saliva just about running down my chin because I was so delighted.

'Did you really, Greg?'

'Sure.'

'You didn't, you know.' She made a clicking sound with her tongue. 'You'd given up hope of ever seeing it.'

'I hadn't really. It was just . . .'

'I've got to unload my groceries.' She moved through into the kitchen. 'And get Clare out of bed.'

I stood back and looked at my board, drank in the fine shape and the very sleekness of it. 'It looks like a great day for surf, down on the beach.'

'There's a breeze, yes.'

'Reckon I'd better go and give her a try now,' I crowed.

'You'll clear up that mess first.'

That was predictable.

'Can't I do it when I come back?'

'That means not at all. You'll do it now.'

'Aw, Mum . . .'

'I'm not going off leaving the place looking like the inside of a warehouse, just because your Dad's not here.'

'All right.'

It was wasting precious surfing time, but it had to be done. I started gathering up the bits, but hardly looked away from the board as I did so.

Then I noticed a manilla foolscap envelope. It was slightly torn and there was Scotch tape on it. Apparently the envelope had been stuck to the board but had been ripped off during my frenzied unpacking.

My fingers fumbled about inside and I came out with a folded piece of paper. There was the name of the surfboard firm at the top, and some figures and writing underneath.

Surely they didn't want me to pay extra money. I was all set to groan.

But no. The amount was the exact price I had paid. Just a delivery note.

The writing said briefly:

Regret delay in forwarding article as ordered. Unprecedented demand—sold out of bargain boards—this one made up specially for you in our finest quality materials. Hoping for your further patronage....

Made up specially!

'Stupenderlous!' I screeched.

'Now what's got you?' said Mum.

'Custom built! My board was custom built.'

I folded up the note and put it in my pocket, my hands trembling with new pleasure.

'Custom built?' It seemed that Mum was as bewildered as ever. 'Now what would that be meaning?'

'It means ... it means.' I chuckled like a miser thinking about his treasures. 'It means everything's fine, that's all. They built the board specially for me, to suit my height and weight, and didn't charge any extra.'

I went into my room with the surfboard. The room was so tiny that the board seemed to fill it. I put some newspaper on the floor, then sprayed the board with gold paint, and coated with resin.

If Nick Hirst saw me around he would know at last that I hadn't just been boasting.

The paint was soon dry. I did some clearing up, then grabbed a towel and put on my swimming shorts. Into my pocket I put my last dollar and a piece of surfer's wax to rub on the board. On the end of my nose I smeared a blob of Mum's sun cream.

'I'm going now,' I called out.

Clare, sleeping late because the holidays had started, was roused by my voice. Tired-eyed, she came stumbling out of her room. 'What's all the racket?'

'My board,' I told her. 'I got it.'

Clare examined it. 'Not bad.'

'Great, that's all.'

'Lucky old Greg.'

'I'll teach you how to ride someday, when you're older.'

'If you're going, Greg, get going,' said Mum. 'And Clare, it's time you had your cereals.'

'Wish I had a surfboard,' said Clare. 'Or a bike, or a dog, or a pony, or a palace.'

'Just for now, you'll have to make do with cereals,' I said.

'And one thing, Greg,' said Mum.

'Well, Mum?' I said.

'Please don't do anything too risky. Don't go too far out. Don't try to be too clever.'

'I won't.'

'If you—or Clare for that matter—start doing crazy things down on the beach while Dad's away, then we'll move away to somewhere safer. Remember.'

'Oh, Mum . . .'

'It's why we should have gone anyway.'

'All right,' I said. 'For Dad's sake if nobody else's.'

'So take care. And don't forget to have it registered.'

'I'll be careful, don't worry.'

She smiled, but it was a worried sort of smile. 'Goodbye then.'

'See ya,' I said.

Clare screamed something after me. It sounded like: 'Lucky for some people.'

Mum had closed the door by now so it was no use shouting anything back. But I said to myself as I went out of the gate: Maybe I'm lucky. But it's what I worked for. It's just what I earned.

As I balanced the board on my head and walked down towards the beach it felt as if everyone was staring at me. I hoped that some of my mates would see me with my golden surfboard. And I hoped that the ones who already had boards of their own would know that I was on equal terms with them now, while the ones without them would be more than a bit envious.

Yet I was all of a shiver.

The big worry was about how I would manage to perform when it came to the testing time out there on the surf. It was going to be very different from riding on a skateboard or a foam-board or a surfoplane.

Suddenly I found myself wishing that I had made a bigger effort to learn the skills beforehand. It would have been sensible for me to borrow a proper board from someone, then I could have sneaked a few practice rides without being conspicuous. At least that would have broken me in a bit for what now seemed to be like a trial by ordeal.

But I had been too proud to beg a ride from somebody with his own board.

And now I was scared like I had never been scared before.

FOURTEEN

THE BOY WITH THE GOLDEN SURFBOARD

It had been a big fear of mine that when the surfboard finally arrived the weather conditions would be wrong for good waves.

The fear was for nothing.

That day the morning was bright and warm. The breeze grew stronger, stirring up some hollow-shaped waves.

Already the whole suburb was swarming with kids of all ages and all sizes, plus the usual few older people who seemed to make the beach their life's background. Everyone seemed to be bustling down to fool around on the sand, or to swim, or to ride skidboards or bellyboards or surfoplanes or surf-skis or boards the style of my own.

I stood near the top of the concrete steps that led down on to the beach proper. My arms ached. I rested my board against the wall, feeling embarrassed.

There was a part of me that wanted everyone to gape with envy at my new board, and another part that wanted no mates to be around so that I could sneak in unnoticed. It seemed that the quiet way in was going to be most likely, for in the muddle of people around I couldn't see anyone I knew by name.

Look at me, thought the side that wanted publicity. *Look at me, look at me, look at me.*

No one seemed to look. All the people seemed to be too busy with their own affairs.

All right then, don't look.

And they didn't.

I hoisted up the surfboard on my head again, with the towel draped over my shoulder, and made my way down the concrete steps, then across the hot sand towards the section of the beach where the board riders were.

The surf was about medium height. That was O.K. for what I needed. It was not glassy, though. Rather uneven. Nothing to terrify anybody, but commanding respect.

I waited, still looking round for familiar faces. Where was Jiranek now? There must have been fifty or more board riders in the water, apart from the hoard in various positions on the beach. I could stay lost among them all until I got used to the idea of being a board-owner.

Over to the left, a surf lifesaving team was going through a practice drill, doing some very smooth overhead running of the line. I wanted to join a junior rescue team as soon as there was a vacancy, so I had a good excuse for watching the real work.

There were also two crews launching their surfboats, and finding it difficult going. A number of kids were watching them. Some people thought the

boats were out-of-date but they were great to watch.

With so many interesting things to be seen around the beach I felt justified in hesitating at the water's edge. Yet the longer I stood there the harder it was going to be to take that first plunge with the board. I realised this but still I didn't make the necessary move.

The boat crews were great to watch. They had a terrible time over the first fifty yards or so, till they were out beyond the turbulence near the shore. One straight-on wave would be half climbed when another sideways-on would catch them and push them off course. Then another would come. And another. Yet they kept going.

The cove with the steering oar, in his precarious perch at the stern, would almost be thrown out but somehow would recover his balance and stick to a task that seemed superhuman, keeping the 26-foot boat right way up.

The shoulder muscles of the crew stood out wet and gleaming in the glare of the sunlight that bounced off the waves.

How sissy I seemed, standing there shivering despite the heat, doing nothing about getting my golden board into the surf. You goat, I thought. Get into the water and once you're in there everything will be all right.

So I steadied my nerves by rubbing some wax on to the board. At least that would make sure I had a good footing when I finally got around to trying a ride. But all my muscles seemed to ache with stiffness as I tried to set myself moving into the ocean.

Now, along the edge of the water, there came some familiar characters who at that moment seemed sinister. Jiranek was one of them. He wasn't so bad, but with him was Nick Hirst, and there was an older cove they called Cass. He had left school but didn't seem to work at anything, just hung around the beach yet wasn't a genuine surf fanatic.

'Look, here's Greg,' said Jiranek, putting his board down on the sand and standing close to it.

'Well, well—Greg's got himself a board,' said Cass in an exaggerated friendly voice. He had enormous pimples, more pimples than face it seemed, and he had an awkward gangly body with a black mop of hair stuck on the top.

'Yes, Greg's got himself a board,' said flabby old Hirst.

'Nice board,' said Cass.

'Yes, nice board,' said Hirst.

'Very nice board,' said Jiranek. There were drops of salt water still clinging to his hair. 'It's a real flat-bottomed, high-nosed beauty. Not as good as my board, but not bad either. Well waxed and everything.'

'And all that lovely gold dazzling our eyes,' said Hirst.

Cass had to assert himself. He said: 'It could do with being baptised, eh, Nick?'

'Sure needs a dip,' agreed Nick Hirst.

'Mine's had a dip,' said Jiranek.

'Why aren't you out in the soup with this lovely golden surfboard?' said Hirst.

'Yairs, why aren't you out there?'

'Are you some kind of chicken or what-not?'

I tried to smile. 'I'm not in any hurry,' I said.

'He's in no hurry,' said Cass in a mocking way as if he was passing on some astonishing information to the others.

'He should be,' said Hirst. 'The off-shore breeze might drop this afternoon.'

'It might rain this afternoon.'

'There might be an earthquake somewhere.'

'Better get working if you want to be a 300-point champ.'

'Yairs, better get working, Sport.'

'Better had, Greg,' said Jiranek, 'or Nat Young and Keith Paull will be old men before you can challenge them.'

Cass stroked the gold lacquer on my board with his finger tips, looking at me through screwed up eyes. His mouth was set in a tantalising smile. 'And the board's already waxed for action, eh?'

'Look, a stringer down the middle,' said Hirst. 'Just great.'

'You know,' said Cass, 'I might just be willing to take her out for you. There wouldn't be any freak-out with me doing the riding.'

'I wouldn't like that,' I said in the boldest voice I could muster.

'Hm . . . Wouldn't like that, Greg boy?'

'No,' I said, 'I wouldn't want the board to get dirty.'

Suddenly, from his slow smooth sidling sarcasm, that Cass galoot switched to abrupt action. Within a few seconds he had hoisted up the board and was manhandling it away into the water.

'No you don't,' I screeched as I started after him.

'Yes I do,' said Cass with a nasty kind of joy.

Hirst laughed, making a lot of noise about it.

'Drop my board,' I shouted.

By now Cass was about fifteen yards into the water.

'Drop it,' I shouted again.

'Drop it, drop it, drop it,' he echoed.

'Give it back to me.'

'No, you said drop it. O.K., man. I'll drop it.'

And Cass gave my surfboard, that golden board I had worked so hard to get, an enormous topple towards the sea. Then, as I stumbled to recover it, the lousy galoot splashed his way past me towards the shore.

I looked all around to see if there was anybody I could find for an ally. Not a chance. Everybody around that place seemed to be interested in their own activities, and if anybody heard the hoo-hah we probably gave the impression of being just some unruly kids indulging in a lot of horseplay.

So I shouted abuse at Cass, then splutteringly I plunged forward as the board was being swirled away. My left hand managed to catch hold of one of the skegs, which felt sharp enough to slash through my fingers.

I wouldn't let go. In the end I lay across the board and somehow forced it back into shallower water.

The other three stood there and laughed.

'Shut your faces,' I spluttered. 'Shut your faces or I'll ...'

'You'll what?' said Hirst. 'You'll call your Dad, maybe?'

The taunt hit me hard. Hirst knew my Dad had cleared off. Cass got the message fast enough, and he laughed all the louder.

'You bunch of no-hopers!' I yelled. 'Why don't you clear off now? You've had your bit of fun, so get lost.'

I was ankle-deep in water, holding my precious board under my arm.

'Why don't you show us a few tricks now your board's wet,' teased Cass. 'If it really is your own board.'

My hands tightened into fists. 'You know too right it is.'

'Sure you didn't steal it?'

'Fair go, Cass,' interrupted Jiranek. 'The kid worked for it.'

'I worked for it,' I snapped. 'No one can take it away.'

I turned back towards the surf. Better to face that than have those galahs squawking lies at me. The trouble is, even an expert can't rush things. And I was no expert ... yet.

I tried to remember things I had learned. Putting the nose of the board into the water, I kept a tight grip on the rails. I slithered on from the rear and lay belly-flat along the centre. Then I started to paddle.

The water was choppy, so I eased back a bit,

bringing the nose up a few inches out of the water.

Now and again I rested from paddling. The surf-board wobbled. I was scared it would topple me into the water. The temptation was to look round and see if the tormentors were still watching, but that would have been disastrous.

It was fair enough to assume that my every move was being watched and commented upon.

I stuck to my task.

At this stage I didn't dare to knee-paddle, though my chest was already sore and it would have been good to advance to my knees. Yet I just couldn't take the chance of being flung off the board.

By now I was in the worst of the white water and getting over too near to the riders coming on the inward run. My arms kept flailing into the surf. I shut my eyes more than once and said some kind of prayer.

Then, strangely, I discovered that I was beyond the rough wake, out where there were no white tops on the waves and there was only the rise and fall of the incoming swell. I had never been out this far before. It was a peculiar feeling and all I wanted to do for a while was just to drift, kicking one foot and then the other to keep the nose of the board pointing seaward.

Out here I felt unusually safe, away from the hurly-burly of the lads on the beach and the rat-race for impressing people with a flashy new possession. Here it was enough to feel the buoyancy of the board underneath me and to know that if the need arose I had the strength and ability to swim and body-surf to safety.

The quiet feeling didn't last long. Almost before I knew it I had drifted back almost to the point where the waves gathered power and momentum, rising high and ready to break.

It was a struggle to swing the board round quickly so that the nose was pointing in the right direction for the return trip.

Now I paddled again and flipped my feet about to set the course straight. Yet when the Big Feller caught me I was not in the best of positions, and the sheer violence of it made me conscious of the breakfast I had not enjoyed that morning.

Panic took control.

I tried to stand up on the board, as if there was a hope of riding in properly at the first attempt. Some people have done it. Not me.

The wave had me completely at its mercy. It was almost as if I had insulted it by thinking I could ride it without having all the know-how and the grace and the sheer brute strength. It seemed as if it wanted to teach me a lesson.

In no time at all an enormous chunk of water slapped me hard over the head and shoulders, and all at once the board nosedived as if a brake had been put on. I was sent spinning to my right. Only instinct made me turn the fall into a half-dive, aiming deep down where the spinning board wouldn't hack at me as if to cut me in two.

I hadn't taken a breath and my lungs felt as if they would collapse under the strain. The swirling water pressed down on me, driving me this way then that way until I forced myself to open my eyes and see the vague, reassuring light somewhere above my head.

It seemed like a week before I broke the surface. There were only a few seconds for me to gulp in air then I had to dive off left to dodge a board-rider who was so close that I could hear the swish of the spray he stirred up, halfway down the wall on the following wave.

Hitting the surface again, I managed to look towards the shore again. The choppy water twenty yards away was thrashing my board around till it was lost in the soup.

It was a nerve-racking swim for me, heading back into shallow water. I was glad to get there without being donged on the head by anyone else's surf-board.

The bright gold showed up near the beach, fortunately. My board was in the shallows, fin uppermost. I examined it with trembling hands, but there were no dings anywhere on it.

I put it on my head and waded out on to the shore, then sank down on the soft sand, fighting to get my breath and shivering all over.

Soon I looked about me to see if Jiranek, Hirst, or Cass had lingered around in a spot where they could watch me. There was no sign of them, but I noticed there was a beach inspector looking at me. He seemed to be staring with more than average curiosity.

I turned away and looked at the ocean. Then I

looked back at the inspector.

He was still eyeing me up and down.

It made me feel horribly uncomfortable, wondering what I had done wrong.

FIFTEEN

TROUBLE IN THE SUN

After about two minutes of taking it easy I felt a lot better. I filled my lungs with air three or four times before standing up.

I looked all around me once again. The three tormentors were not in view. The inspector had gone.

I walked thirty or forty yards along the beach and found my thongs and towel half-buried in the sand. After I had slipped my feet into the thongs I squeaked my way over the burning sand towards the steps.

Now I knew what I would do . . .

At the top of the steps my sister was waiting for me. I hadn't recognised her until I was almost a foot or two away, because she was wearing that floppy red sun-hat and her face was in a dark shadow.

'Hi, Greg!' she cooed.

'Hi, Clare,' I answered.

'You look all knocked out, Greg.'

'I feel fine.'

'You don't look fine.'

'Never mind that, just tell me what you're doing down here all on your own. Does Mum know?'

'She said I could stand at the top of the steps near the surf sheds and no further.'

Somebody jostled me. I swung my board round to let them pass. 'I'm not staying here,' I told Clare.

'I just thought you looked dead on your feet.'

'I'm fine, I tell you.'

'Where are you going, then?'

'To another beach.'

'Why not here? You like Bondi best.'

'It's crowded right now,' I explained, but it was a sort of lie because it wasn't too bad, considering the holidays.

'Which beach are you going to?'

'Tamarama.'

'What will you do there?'

I didn't answer, but thought about my plan.

The plan was that I should do some board-riding practice in the more secluded bay at Tamarama, then in a few days time I would start riding back at Bondi and dazzle people like Jiranek with my skill.

'What will you do there?' repeated Clare.

'Try a few tricks.'

'Can I come with you?'

'No, Clare, you can't.'

'Aw, Greg . . .'

'Nothing doing.'

'Go on. I've got my own spending money to get there.'

'Like I said once, no.'

'Mum won't mind, while she's working at the fruit shop.'

'She wouldn't like it. She'd go crook on me if I took you to Tamarama.'

'If you don't take me,' sulked Clare, 'I won't be your friend any more.'

'All right, so be my enemy. I reckon everybody else is.'

'Nuts.'

She pulled the sun-hat lower over her head with a show of anger I didn't see often. Her mouth was set in a pout.

I managed to smile at her. 'Go back to Mum at the fruit shop. Maybe she'll take you to the baths for a swim this arvo.'

'Boys have all the luck. Why can't I have a golden surfboard?'

'Come on, Clare. You've got to get going.'

We walked up over the lawns towards home, me with my board balanced on my head and Clare scraping her feet along behind her. I crossed her over Campbell Parade to the safe side.

'Aw, Greg,' she pleaded in a last big effort, 'can't I come and see you to your board-riding?'

'Go to Mum,' I snapped, toughening my attitude to her.

'Mum's busy working.'

'Go on.'

'Nobody wants me.'

'Course they do,' I said, resting my board against my shoulder.

'My Dad would.'

'He's in the Snowy Mountains.'

'I want my Dad.'

I gave her a gentle nudge in the direction of the fruit shop. 'Get going, Clare.'

Her pleading faded away in a muddle of traffic noises as I crossed over, board on head, and moved away in the direction of Tamarama. Sam Rukovski was near the bus-stop. He was sitting on his bike, one foot propped against the kerb. I didn't want him to see me . . . yet.

On impulse I hailed a blue cab. It was one of three or four cruising along empty at what seemed to be a slack time of day. In a casual way the driver strapped my board on top, fins uppermost, and whisked me inside before Sam even got around to glancing my way.

I felt a spasm of fear. It was a fear that I had got into the cab without having any money. People like Hirst had enough cash to be able to jump into cabs whenever they felt like it, but it was only the third time in my life I had even ridden in one, let alone on my own.

In a flurry I groped into the little pocket of my beach shorts, still damp from my trip into the surf. The dollar I had wrapped in the picnic paper was still there, fortunately.

Now I sat back, but felt mean because I was travelling in a kind of luxury style while Dad was away at the Snowy, sweating away to improve our financial position.

Ah well, I thought as the cab moved away from Bondi, it's not every day a bloke gets a brand new surfboard.

If I had walked all the way to Tamarama, board on head, it would have taken quite a while. But in the blue cab, with my board strapped on the rack, I was there in a few minutes.

The surf looked big in Tamarama, but this was because the rocky outcrops on each side made everything on such a smaller scale. If anything the waves weren't so tough because on that day there was more shelter than at Bondi.

There was no one around that I recognised, and when I had paid the cab-driver and was walking down the steep path to the narrow little beach there was a wonderful sense of being free. Now I wouldn't have to do big things so as to avoid being tormented.

I spent twenty minutes, perhaps, just paddling my board in and out, not too far from the shoreline. This way I got to know the board better and I liked to think it was getting to know me. I found the best way to launch the board without getting the skeg trapped in the sand while still in shallow water. I found the best place for my body to be to balance the board, and even located a tiny red patch which was the best point for my chin to be over.

No longer was there any tension in my body. The panicky time I'd had during the episode back at my favourite beach was almost forgotten.

After a spell I decided I would take a rest in the sun then continue the paddling practice.

I found a spot near the refreshment hut. Now to

relax, I thought. But there was a familiar voice.
'Hey there, Greg!'

It was Sam calling. He was on the twisting pathway, up above me.

Oh no, I thought.

I looked up. Sam was looking down at me. He had one hand supporting his flashy bike.

'Get lost,' I said, not too loudly.

Whether Sam heard the insult or not was hard to say, but he shouted:

'Greg, you've got to come up here right away.'

There was something about the way in which he said it that made me choke back the other words of abuse beginning to form in my mouth.

'What is it?' I called back as I hoisted up my board and my towel, and started the upward trudge.

'Nick Hirst, for one thing,' he said when I was closer to him.

'Hirst?' I said, baffled.

'He's been venting his spite on you.'

'How do you mean, venting his spite?'

I propped my board against a rock at the side of the cliff path.

'Well,' said Sam, 'you know that there's been a big hoo-hah at Bondi about the missing surfboards?'

'Who doesn't?' I said. 'It was in the paper, for one thing.'

'Nick Hirst has played a stinking trick on you. He's told a surf club bloke that you were mixed up in stealing the surfboards. Apparently somebody even saw you putting a board on top of a cab and riding away. That increased their suspicions.'

I just about hit the sky. 'That's my board I had with me. Look at it—gold along the rails.'

And I tapped the gold part with pride.

'Don't scream at me,' said Sam. 'I didn't have anything to do with these stupid accusations.'

'That Nick Hirst! Just wait till I catch up with him.'

'More important than that is that the bloke is out searching for you. Dellinger, they call him. A big bloke in a maroon nylon jacket. Better keep a good look-out, Greg.'

When I touched my new board I could have cried. My board, it was. Nobody else's. If Hirst had fixed things so that they took the board away from me, and got me dubbed as a thief into the bargain, life was going to be hell.

'Worse still to come,' said Sam, taking a look over his shoulder.

'There can't be anything worse than that lot,' I said.

'There is, Greg—though I had to give you the tip-off about that Dellinger bloke first.'

'Come on, then. Tell me.'

'It's about Clare,' he said.

'What about Clare?'

He sure looked worried. 'Well, she's only seven, isn't she?'

'What are you getting at?' I asked in a peevish way.

'Setting out on her own to come to Tam-arama . . .'

'Clare . . . coming here?'

'That's what the kid said she was going to do, back at Bondi.'

There was a sick feeling that seemed to reach from my stomach to my throat. 'Couldn't you have stopped her?'

Sam was indignant. 'What, grab her, you mean? Look, kids her age are slippery as flatheads. Told me she was going where she could be with Greg, then she was off and lost in the crowd.'

'Which way do you reckon she took?'

'Along the top of the cliff, maybe, although I didn't pass her along the road anywhere. Could be on the path . . . or she could have taken the bus.'

I shouldn't have been scowling at him. He was still covered in sweat after the fast ride from Bondi. He couldn't have done more.

'No use me still standing here,' I moaned. 'I'll have to go and look for her.'

'I'll pedal back along the road,' said Sam. 'Maybe I will see her along there.'

What I said next took a lot of saying. Maybe it even meant goodbye to living at the beach. 'Get Mum from the fruit shop, Sam. She's got to know sooner or later.'

He saw the pained look on my face but said: 'O.K., Greg, I'll warn her.'

He jumped on to his bike and pedalled off up the hill, calling out: 'And watch out for that bloke in the maroon jacket.'

'I will,' I answered. 'And thanks.'

I don't think he heard, but my mind was too

much on putting my surfboard into safe hands while I searched for Clare along the cliffs. It was too heavy to carry at speed along the rugged path. I just couldn't take a chance if I was going to find her before she became lost, or even hurt.

Close by, at the top of the cliff, there was a white-haired man sitting in a deck-chair outside an old brick house.

I stumbled along the path in that direction. The sweat was pouring down my face because of fear and anxiety in the humid conditions. Two people abused me for almost bumping into them with my board, but I puffed my way to the spot where the white-haired man was slumped down in his deck-chair, a can of beer at his side.

He was a cheerful old fellow.

When he heard that I was going to look for a missing girl he agreed to keep an eye on my surf-board. He smiled as he looked at the golden lacquer I had sprayed on the board. He told me to put the board inside the garden wall.

I suppose I said thanks, then off I went at an agonised trot in the direction of Bondi.

I didn't get far.

A sunbaked hand reached out from behind a wall and grabbed me by the left wrist. I spun and slithered about, trying to break free. But the pain of the firm grip was too much and I looked up into the face of a grim-eyed, black-haired man.

'Hold on, Goofy-foot!' he rasped at me.

'I've got to get going,' I said.

He was wearing a maroon-coloured nylon jacket

so I knew then I must be looking at the man I had been warned about. Dellinger, that's what Sam had called him.

'You're not going anywhere yet,' the man said, forcing me into the shelter of a secluded gateway.

There were people not far away, yet I was reluctant to yell for help because people meant a delay to looking for Clare, and I was convinced that they were only too ready to think I'd done wrong.

The man seemed to sense that I was scared to call out. His dark, angry eyes seemed to get larger. I could feel the sweat from his hand on my wrist, but he would not relax that vicious grip.

'Please, mister,' I begged, 'you must have got hold of the wrong story somewhere.'

'The usual tale,' he snapped. 'Look, Goofy-foot, I've been watching you. Now I know where you've been getting rid of these stolen surfboards.'

'Hirst must have lied to you about me.'

'Hirst? If I've got hold of the wrong story, how did you know anything about him telling me?'

I couldn't involve Sam in this trouble, so I kept quiet about him. 'I've got to get going,' I said again. 'Got to.'

Dellinger still would not let go of me, but I did feel a slight decrease in the pressure on my wrist and the hand was even more slippery with sweat.

My feeling of desperation grew. There were so many fears in my mind ... the fear of losing my precious golden board ... the fear of trouble through being labelled a thief ... the fear of having to shift house from the beach.

But at that time the worst fear of all was not finding Clare.

'If my Dad was here now,' I spluttered, 'he'd show you . . .'

In a rush of strength I tried to wrench myself free of the man in the maroon jacket. The shock of this new effort made him spin back towards the gate.

At last I had a hand free. The flesh on my wrist still stung. The pain made me all the more determined when he lunged back at me.

My fingers clawed at him. One of them stabbed into his right eye.

Dellinger reeled away, grunting like a hog, groping to try and soothe himself where it hurt.

Just outside the gate he overbalanced. All around me things blurred, but I saw him topple backwards against the wall.

There was a nasty thud.

Silence for a few moments.

Now my own footsteps, taking me away from the scene as fast as possible with the clumsy thongs slip-slopping under me.

A man's voice from somewhere behind me, shouting abuse. At me, most likely.

The distance widening between me and the gateway where the man in the maroon jacket had tried to make me into a kind of prisoner. Sweat and dust almost blinding my eyes . . .

I kept going, determined more than ever that I would find Clare.

SIXTEEN

BLUNDER

I kept moving as fast as I could until I reached a point where the path left the road on the right.

There I halted. Until my breathing evened out again I could travel no further.

I looked back. There was no sign of anyone following, and just at that time there was hardly anybody around.

With my breath almost back to normal but my heart still pumping like fury I set off northwards along the path. As I went I found myself wondering about Sam, and whether he had got as far as seeing Mum by this time.

There were three teenage girls coming towards me dolled up in beach gear, and they were giggling about something they seemed to think was funny. I spluttered out a question about Clare, describing her as fast as I could.

No, they hadn't seen her, so one told me. They carried on in the direction of Tamarama, giggling louder than ever.

'Sheilas,' I moaned. 'Just crazy.'

The sun was low, yet the air was stifling. Sweat

from my hair trickled down into my eyes.

I forced myself to keep going. Somewhere between there and Bondi my sister was maybe lost or hurt, with no one around to help her. Now, despite all my worry about my surfboard and Dellinger and moving away from the beach, most of all I was worried about Clare.

From where I was now I couldn't see the road which bent off inland from the coast, so I had to hope I wasn't missing Sam along that way. It must have been another three hundred yards or so along that I saw something which compelled my attention, and put a sharp edge to all my fears.

There was a splash of red near the clifftop. Something like a sun-hat, I reckoned. Clare's hat, maybe.

I stumbled forward and grabbed at the object. It wasn't a sun-hat, it was just the wrapping from a food package. I flung it down, angry at being deceived yet glad that it wasn't evidence of Clare falling over the cliff.

Looking down at the rocks far below, I saw that there was no sign of her anyhow. Yet I had to puzzle out where she had taken herself off to.

I looked along the cliff path, both ways.

When I turned my head to the south I saw two men heading my way. Perhaps they had something to do with Dellinger and him striking his head against the wall. If I let them get too close they might drag me off somewhere without allowing me to make a proper search for Clare.

I couldn't risk that. Turning towards Bondi, I

set off at a run along the clifftop.

Maybe I slowed down for a few yards now and again on the way, but it didn't seem like it. By the time I reached the rugged part some people call The Boot, I just had to stop and fill my lungs with air. The breeze at the south end of the Bay was a welcome aid to revival, and I leaned against a rock to snatch some energy back.

I looked behind me, along the path towards Tamarama. The two men were nowhere to be seen. Perhaps I had moved too fast for them, or I was mistaken about them following me. Either way, it was a relief.

To my right, the surf was pounding against the rocks at the bottom of the cliff. The thought of it set my muscles shivering. Had I missed Clare somewhere along the way? Was she down at the bottom, limp and helpless, perhaps already in the grip of the ocean?

It was away from the road here, and there was no Sam to help me in the search. I had to move myself.

Just as well I did. Clare was around the next corner, standing there on the ugliest rock, right above a jutting-out piece of cliff.

'Clare!' I called.

But she didn't hear. It was the breeze and the sound of the waves, muffling my voice.

I had to force myself not to rush in her direction. She was so near the edge that a sudden movement might startle her into going over.

I walked slowly towards the rock. The impression was that she was hypnotised by the movement of the water below. You can feel like that if you stand at the side of a moving ship, looking down. You sometimes feel that if you slide down into the sea you could swim for ever.

Anyway, the thought of all this was enough to make me approach her very cautiously.

When I was only about ten feet away from her she turned, and suddenly her gloomy face went very bright. 'Greg,' she said, 'I thought I'd never see you again.'

I moved forward and grabbed her by the arm. Fortunately she didn't squirm or get awkward in any way.

I eased her away from the edge of the rock. There was a vacant look in her eyes now, almost as if it didn't occur to her how dangerous it was for her to stand on the cliff, as if she felt it was possible to stand near the edge all evening and all night without falling over.

'You should have stayed home, or at the shop,' I scolded.

'It was you I was worried about,' said Clare. 'First I just wanted to see you ride your golden surfboard. Then I got worried that you'd been riding the waves down here, but had been in a big wipe-out on the rocks. I thought you were dead.'

'Other way round,' I said.

She smiled, the cutest little reassuring smile. 'I was all right.'

I let go of her arm, she seemed so composed.

'But where's your golden board?' she went on.

'Did you lose it in the surf?'

At last I managed to grin. Clare was as worried about my board as I was. Rapidly I explained to her about Sam coming to Tamarama, and about the man called Dellinger, and about leaving the surfboard at a stranger's house.

'But we've got to go right now and get your board,' she protested. 'What are we standing here for, Greg? Let's get going.'

I chewed at my lip. What I knew was that I ought to take Clare home first. Mum would be worried about her. And somehow I saw all this as one more black mark against living at the beach. This could be the final event that would make Mum move us away.

'We'll go home first,' I said.

'No,' said Clare. 'The golden surfboard first, then home.'

'Mum will go crook on me if you don't get back soon.'

'Mum will go crook on you if you go home without that surfboard you paid so much for,' she reasoned.

Heck, I did want to go and get the board. I didn't want to be away from it. When I had it back I would keep it in my room at night and wake up in the wee small hours and touch it to make sure it was still there.

But now I was still standing there, in a kind of limbo between Bondi and Tamarama, not doing anything.

Clare grabbed my hand and urged me towards

the south, where my golden surfboard was. 'For goodness' sake come on, Greg. While we're standing here arguing, we could be halfway to Tamarama.'

'All right,' I said, and we set off at a cracking pace.

Perhaps, I thought, we would see Sam along the road, and he could let Mum know Clare was O.K. Perhaps Mum herself might have come looking for us, so everything would be all right.

We didn't see Sam. We didn't see Mum. And by the time we got back to Tamarama we were both just about dead-beat. It was a sticky, humid evening, with a short dusk that meant it was almost dark.

Almost dark! Oh heck, I thought, that's going to start Mum getting all the more worried, as Clare wasn't home.

At last we were at the old brick house where the white-haired man lived. Everything was gloomy round there, and few people seemed to be around now the surfing day was over and dusk had put a stop to activities round one of the quietest beaches in Sydney.

At first the whole place seemed to be in darkness. Clare shuddered. She was used to the bright lights that lit the evenings around Bondi. 'It's spooky,' she said.

Just then there was a glimmer of light at the back of the house. It was enough to illuminate the place where my surfboard had been propped up against the garden wall. No sign of a golden gleam there.

I forced myself not to get too anxious as I went with Clare to the front door and rang the bell.

An age seemed to pass, with me listening intently and Clare whispering now and again that she thought she could hear something. At last the door opened and the old man appeared, peering at us in the vague light from the hallway.

'Oh,' he said, 'it's you at last, and it looks as if you were successful in finding your sister.'

I nodded, then gave a nervous gulp. 'My board . . . what about that?'

'Are you all right, young lady?' he asked Clare, ignoring my concern about the surfboard.

Clare nodded.

'That's good,' he said.

He kept peering at us, and I thought he was never going to say anything about the golden surfboard.

'Can I have it back?' I said after a while.

'Oh, your surfboard. Well, yes . . .'

Even now he made no move to indicate where it was. I looked at him, then at Clare, finally back at the place where I had leaned it against the wall. 'It isn't where I put it,' I told the old man.

'No,' he answered, suddenly brightening up as if in recollection. 'It's where I put it. Er . . . in the garage.'

I sighed, not disguising my relief. 'Fine,' I said.

But he didn't make any kind of move to lead the way to the garage. He looked kind of scared. Was he absent-minded, nervous because of getting on a bit in years, or was there some hint of suspicion perhaps about the surfboard being stolen—the results of hearing things on the radio? I couldn't make up my mind.

'Would you like me to get the surfboard from the garage?' I suggested awkwardly.

He nodded, and fumbled for some switch in the porch. A brilliant light flooded the dark patch at the side of the house. The old man now led the way to the garage.

He spent what seemed like ages rummaging through his pockets for the key. It almost seemed as if he was deliberately playing for time. I glanced towards the gateway, with an uncomfortable feeling that somebody might be watching us.

Next thing I knew the doors were open, and there was my golden board, propped up against the wall next to the old man's Valiant.

Clare suddenly became very excited, and took a good deal of pleasure in helping me to ease it out on to the driveway. I was relieved to discover that there were no dings in it despite the cramped stowage space.

'Anyhow, thanks for looking after it, mister,' I said.

He watched as I took the board in my arms, with Clare running her fingers along its smooth surface.

I was thinking about my clash with Dellinger, and how he might have been able to tell me something of the outcome—how badly hurt he was. I somehow didn't have the courage to raise the subject, but as it happened the white-haired man broached the subject.

'Take care on your way home, you two,' he warned. 'Some person got involved in a fight just up the road while you were searching for your sister. You never know who you're going to meet up with these days.'

'We'll be careful,' I promised.

'Got attacked from behind, he did, not long after you left here. Or so he said. Can't tell these days . . .'

'Was he all right?'

'Who?' said the old man, absent-minded as ever.

'The bloke in the fight. Was he badly hurt?'

'Not badly, no. Maybe he'd done too much boozing, and started being hostile to somebody bigger than himself.'

That's a laugh, I thought. Somebody bigger!

'Well, thanks again,' I said out loud. 'And we've not been boozing.'

'Just take care, that's all.'

I gave my surfboard a big hitch, clear from the ground, then led Clare off towards Bondi.

'Now we've nothing to worry about,' said Clare happily. 'You've got the golden board, and I reckon Mum won't go too crook on us once she sees I'm all right.'

'There's plenty to worry about, apart from Mum taking us away from the house at the beach,' I assured her as we trudged through the gloom. And I explained a lot more about Dellinger and the accusations about the stolen surfboards. 'For a while I thought that old man in there had confis-

134

cated the golden board, thinking I had pinched it,'
I wound up.

'Never mind,' said Clare, 'I reckon you taught
this Dellinger chap a real lesson. You won't have
to deal with him again.'

'At least the old man back there didn't say he
was badly hurt, and that's one thing I was scared
of most.'

'It would have served him right if he had ended
up in hospital,' she said through a pout.

'Oh, would it?' said a nasty voice to the left of
where we were walking.

Immediately I realised two things. One, we were
near the spot where Dellinger had set about me
earlier on. Two, I recognised the voice as that of
Dellinger himself.

Startled out of her wits, Clare scuttled round to
the other side of me, away from the voice.

We had stopped instinctively.

The nose of my surfboard came to rest on the
footpath, but I didn't let go of the fins even though
Dellinger came out of hiding near the hedge and
grabbed my arm again. He put a kind of lock on
me that made me grunt with the pain.

Dellinger's face looked even more savage in the
dark. His breath told me the old man had been
right about the boozing.

Clare started shivering but said: 'Let go of my
brother, or I'll . . .'

'You'll what?' he snapped. 'You'll nothing!'

Still I wasn't going to let go of my golden surfboard. I was so angry that I said: 'I should have

pushed you harder, I reckon.'

'I reckon there's no convenient wall to help you get away this time,' he answered in a horrible rasping voice.

'I'll yell,' threatened Clare. 'I'll yell blue murder until somebody comes.'

'You'd be foolish to do that,' he said. 'Who's going to come and help a rotten sneak thief?'

'I'm no thief,' I said.

He rapped the knuckles of his free hand hard against my surfboard. 'This board was stolen. You sprayed the gold stuff over it to disguise that.'

I was so furious that I could hardly speak. The short silence which followed seemed to give him self-confidence in the wild accusations. He leaned closer, and tightened the grip on my arm again.

Clare kept up her courage. I had thought that she might run away in terror of Dellinger, but she continued to speak up to him. 'Let go of my brother, I tell you. You've got the wrong person. That board wasn't stolen.'

'Nuts to that,' he said. 'A bloke I know lost a board like this the other day registered at Bondi Beach.'

'It's custom-built,' I spluttered. 'Only just came from Brisbane . . . I was going to register it.'

'That's a proper snake story. Admit it, kid, and I'll ease up on you. Look, from what I've been told, you and your family could never afford a custom-built surfboard. I reckon you haven't even the price of a ticket on the Manly ferry, let alone a beaut thing like this.'

'He earned the money,' sobbed Clare.

'Hard yacker,' I said.

'Delivering papers . . .'

'For months and months . . .'

But Dellinger did not seem to be impressed. If anything his grip was worse. The pain and anger together made my head seem to swirl through a toppling heavy deluge of surf.

'Come on,' he ordered, 'you got to hand over that board now and admit it's not yours. I'll hand it back to my mate at Bondi, you learn your lesson, and that'll be that.'

SEVENTEEN

SAM AGAIN

It was Sam, with the headlight on his bike lighting up the three of us and the board, who brought a touch of hope to a situation that had begun to seem hopeless.

Sam, riding towards us at speed, then slowing down and sizing up the scene in the shortest possible time.

Sam, not saying a word but turning back to pedal even faster in the direction from which he had come.

Chickening out because Dellinger looked such a wild, tough person? No, I didn't think so. Not the Sam of nowadays, with the new-found courage that had come from finding he could succeed at something—namely his bike-riding. I put my trust in Sam.

Momentarily, Dellinger looked extra-furious at being disturbed by the beam of Sam's very lively bike-lamp. Then when Sam pulled away he became a vague, menacing shape again.

'I'm going to have that surfboard now,' he threatened, his voice boozier than ever.

'You're not,' I assured him.

He grabbed hold of the fin, at the same time not letting go of my arm. I twisted about furiously, and hacked at the hand that was clutching at my surfboard. Dellinger felt the pain, let go of the fin, and now put his other hand to help the one that gripped my arm. He seemed bewildered at meeting all this resistance from somebody much younger than himself. And he seemed so utterly convinced that I was the surfboard thief that he was not prepared to back out of his plan—returning the board to the person he believed was the rightful owner.

The struggle got wilder.

There were curses from Dellinger. More struggling from me. Finally, down went the surfboard on to the footpath. And that, so far as Clare was concerned, was the limit.

All this time she had been getting more and more excited about the way the man was knocking me about. Now she went into action. Usually Clare was a passive sort of girl, not given to the tantrums that some sisters display. On this occasion she seemed to go wild.

It's funny how some families will squabble among themselves day and night, not pulling any punches or sparing any insults. Yet if the same family should be threatened by an outside force, that's a different matter—they will rally to each other even at the expense of personal safety.

Clare kicked Dellinger in the shin with all the force of a Rugby League player kicking the winning goal in a Grand Final. Then she jumped up and clawed at his face.

He let go of me.

I stooped to rescue my surfboard.

He cuffed Clare, and I spiked him with my elbow.

He grabbed at me again. Clare screamed.

Clare bit him on the wrist. He grunted and let go of me. I spiked him again.

The next minute was a whirl of wild activity, with blows and counter-blows, and pulling, and scratching, and grunting, and screeching.

But in the end, Dellinger had a good grip on my surfboard and I was left sprawling on the foot-path with Clare bending over me and trying to help me back into a standing position.

Oh heck, I thought, that Dellinger bloke has got the better of us after all. Goodbye to my golden surfboard. Goodbye to all the efforts of the past months. Goodbye to the green water and the white-topped waves.

Yet I was wrong.

The powerful lights of a car came into view from the direction in which Sam appeared to have fled.

I realised that it was a police prowl-car.

Dellinger realised it too.

He stopped, and rested the surfboard against his shoulder. Somehow I could tell that he expected to be backed up by the police officer when the prowl-car stopped and the officer dismounted.

But to Dellinger's disappointment it didn't work out like that.

'Just hold it there a minute!' the voice of the officer commanded.

Dellinger stood stock-still, the golden board glinting next to him in the brilliant headlights. I struggled to my feet. My vision blurred, then cleared. Clare, game as ever, helped to steady me.

The officer, as tall as Mount Kosiasco, turned out to be one called Sergeant Croxley. He switched off the motor of the prowl-car, then stalked up to Dellinger in a manner that had move-if-you-dare written all over it.

Dellinger still avoided moving. Which was wise, with a hefty officer like Croxley around.

There was another light coming down the road now. Sam was back again on his bike.

'Good old Sam!' I breathed.

'Yes, good old Sam . . .' murmured Clare.

Clare knew, as I knew, that Sam was the one who had brought the police officer to the scene. The car had been searching for Clare along the cliff road.

Dellinger was shocked. He couldn't work out why the police officer was looking at him in a somewhat hostile manner. Sergeant Croxley seemed to be glaring at him in a way that would have defied the devil to make the wrong move.

Dellinger turned back to look at me, and scowled.

I scowled back at Dellinger.

Then I moved towards him and rested my hands on the fins of my golden surfboard. I felt groggy, but somehow I knew that things were going to be all right. 'This surfboard is mine, I tell you,' I said. 'It's mine.'

Sergeant Croxley, close to us now, gave a fierce

glare at Dellinger and moved like a well-oiled machine to stand next to him.

Dellinger, rather limply, said:

'This kid has been involved in a racket of stealing surfboards. I caught him red-handed.'

Slowly, almost without expression, Sergeant Croxley exploded this nasty theory about me being a thief. 'There were complaints, certainly. We have to check up on these things, and we did, golden paint and everything.'

'And what did you discover?' challenged Dellinger.

'We discovered that this kid earned money by doing a paper run, fair and square. He wrote away to Brisbane for this surfboard. It came this morning. He sprayed it with gold. That's all there is to it.'

The man called Dellinger began to look like a tyre that had a puncture. 'Seems I've been led up a blind alley by that kid Hirst, then.'

He looked at me. He could have said sorry. But he didn't. He just shrugged his shoulders and stood there in the gleam of the police-car's headlights, looking as I thought rather stupid.

Sergeant Croxley, arms folded, did not remove his gaze from Dellinger for quite a while. 'Perhaps,' he said, 'this will serve as a lesson to you not to take the law into your own hands in future, but to report things in the proper manner.'

Dellinger, red in the face, protested:

'But the law wasn't doing anything about it, was it?'

A few more people were listening nearby by this time. The white-haired man with whom I had left my surfboard had been attracted by the din. The others were from neighbouring houses.

Occasionally people side up with those who get into trouble with the Law. But not this time. They were against Dellinger. They were on my side, fair and square.

'The Law has done plenty about it,' Sergeant Croxley lectured. 'The Law has found out that this kid had nothing to do with any stolen surfboards. But we're holding a chap who has. He's the one behind the whole business of stolen surfboards, and other sports gear as well . . .'

Clare was looking up at me and smiling.

'This particular chap,' went on Sergeant Croxley, 'told his son to spread it around that this young 'un here was to blame. Naturally the plan was for attention to be drawn away from himself. But we bided our time. We waited. We watched. And then we nabbed him.'

By now I was certain who the sergeant was talking about. Mr Hirst. Nick's dad. Nick was the one who had been spreading the stories about me.

'Hirst . . .' I breathed.

Sergeant Croxley looked at me. He said nothing, for it wasn't right for him to do so. But his eyes told me I was right.

Dellinger knew I was right too. All the stuffing seemed to be knocked out of him now. He had no more to say.

'Gee, thanks, officer,' I said. And I understood

145

why Nick Hirst had always seemed to have plenty of sports gear—because of his father having done the systematic thieving! What a stinking way to make money.

'All right,' said Sergeant Croxley to Dellinger, 'you can beat it. Go and lose yourself somewhere west of Wagga Wagga.'

I could scarcely help chuckling. The sergeant was obviously such a polite man normally, yet here he was putting Dellinger right in his place.

Dellinger, quite defeated, did not look at me any more. He slunk off into the darkness and after that I never ever saw him again.

Now the harshness went out of Sergeant Croxley's voice. He saw the way I had taken hold of the golden surfboard and was almost caressing it. 'Go on, son,' he said, 'take your golden surfboard home, and tomorrow just ride a wave specially for me.'

Well, there seemed nothing much more that Clare or I could say. I smiled at Sam, watching approvingly from the saddle of his bike, and he smiled back at me . . .

'Good old Sam,' I said again.

EIGHTEEN

DECISION

Mum made a great fuss of Clare, because she had been so worried about her going along the cliffs on her own.

Fair enough.

She also made a great fuss of Sam, who had pedalled that bike of his to get some police help when we were in real trouble.

Again, fair enough.

But not me. I got an almighty nagging because of the danger Clare had got herself into. Once again there was talk of leaving Bondi. And I was reminded of Mum's early fears that something terrible would happen if we went to live near the beach. Why, when it had grown dark and Clare was still not home, Mum had even put in a phone call to Cooma with the idea of getting in touch with Dad—she was that worried.

So the joy of being able to come home with my golden surfboard was short-lived.

When I went out next morning I left the board in my room.

That afternoon, though, when I arrived home I

found that Dad had come back from Cooma. The whole house seemed brighter. Clare was sitting by his side and they were chattering away happily. He greeted me casually, but spilled out the story of how Mum's phone call about Clare being missing had made him decide to take the first plane back to Sydney. Some of his mates at the Snowy had chipped in with a few dollars to help out.

Suddenly, then, everything seemed to be all right again. I wanted Dad to come down to the board-riding part of the beach and see the golden surf-board in action.

Then Mum threw iced water over that idea. She was in a mood for talking Dad into taking us all away from the ocean, to live in some place she considered to be safe.

'If we lived somewhere inland we could come here every now and again for a holiday treat, when we could keep a proper eye on Clare and Greg—as we really should do.'

'Not me,' I muttered stubbornly. 'I don't need ...'

'Don't go on about moving again,' Dad was saying. 'And don't worry so much about everything.'

'Somebody has had to do the worrying,' she complained, 'with you off at the Snowy and everything.'

'I'm back now, aren't I?'

'But not to stay.'

'Yes,' he said, 'to stay.'

Clare hugged Dad, and I couldn't help grinning.

'Can we manage?' said Mum. 'Financially, I mean.'

'Well, I haven't earned quite as much dough as I intended. But my pay cheque will be cleared within a day or two. The people at Cooma understand the position, and things have taken a turn for the better back at the old place here in Sydney. I can start first thing Monday, and in the meantime I've saved just enough to clear our immediate debts.'

Even Mum had to smile.

'Can we have a party this arvo, Mum?' begged Clare. 'Just like we did when we first moved into this house!'

'Go on, Mum,' I said.

'Go on,' said Dad.

Reluctantly Mum said all right, but somehow I knew it was going to be a tremendous feed to celebrate Dad coming home.

Just then there was a knock on the door. It sounded like somebody tapping out a tune.

'It's Sam,' I said, and let him in.

'Hi, Greg,' said Sam.

'Hi,' I said.

Mum brought Sam a glass of cordial. He was popular with Mum for two reasons. One, the way he had helped with Clare. Two, he liked bike-riding and being a land sport that was preferable to surfing in Mum's eyes.

Sam had been having a training stint on his bike and he downed the fruit juice in about three gulps.

Dad talked to Sam about his bike-riding, and we all talked about the party.

'So you're going to stay at the beach after all,'

said Sam hopefully.

'I wouldn't say that,' said Mum. 'This lot have been trying to talk me into it, but ever since we came here things seem to have gone wrong.'

'Blame the beach, and that's just like blaming me,' I complained.

'No it isn't, Greg,' she said uneasily, knowing how resentful I was that I should be held responsible for Clare roaming away from home.

'I just hope you Stevens people stay, that's all,' Sam told her.

He looked miserable. He cleared his throat in a self-conscious way.

For once, Mum sat down instead of buzzing around the house. 'Are you trying to say something else, Sam?' she suggested.

'Please don't go, that's all . . .'

'Look, Sam, if we do go, you'll find another friend—perhaps one who likes bike-riding as much as you.'

He gulped.

'Speak up, Sam,' Dad ordered.

Sam looked hard at Mum. 'Well, you see, Mrs Stevens, it's just that I've decided I want to have another go at learning to swim. And I know that if there's one person in the world that can help me, it's Greg.'

Mum was touched, and in rather fumbling words, she said so.

'Maybe it seems a bit like boasting,' Sam went on, 'but I went in for a junior bike race at Moore Park this week, and I won. Just determination, I reckon . . .' He paused, looking embarrassed as we chipped in with some congrats. 'What I'm really getting at is that this has given me the confidence to go in the water again . . . first time since I began High School . . . well, that's if Greg will be around to keep an eye on things . . .'

'Help him, Greg,' said Clare brightly. 'Help Sam.'

Sam Rukovski grinned sheepishly. 'Oh, I could never swim like Greg and all that . . . but just to be able to keep up in the water, and maybe help somebody in trouble someday . . . that's all I . . .'

He got up as if to go.

Mum got up and touched his arm with her hand. Mum was a shy sort of person, and she had to like somebody a whole lot to make any kind of real contact with them. 'You know, sonny,' she said to him, 'you make me feel sort of ashamed, as if you're ready to face up to things, but I'm not . . . in fact I suppose I'm just running blindly away from some phantom I've built up in my mind.'

He looked at me, then back at Mum. 'You're maybe thinking you could stay on at Bondi, then?'

I never heard Mum sigh like she did that day, before answering his question. 'Oh . . . I'm sure I'm outvoted beyond hope. Dad, Greg, Clare . . . and now you, Sam. You young devil!'

'We can stay living at the beach for a while then, Mum?' I said, brightening up a bit.

'For ever, I imagine,' she answered.

NINETEEN

A SLIDE DOWN THE MOUNTAINS OF THE MOON

Now it's a new morning, the last day of the holidays. Back to High School tomorrow, and I'm going to delve like an opal-digger to get some know-how out of those books up there. I sort of owe it to Mum, I reckon.

Yesterday Sam had another swimming lesson, out of sight of the mickey-takers. He puffed and spluttered, indicating that his real strength still lies in bike-riding, and always will. Yet he'll make some kind of swimmer one day, will Sam, because he has the right amount of determination.

Clare is all smiles these days, and skips around the beach full of confidence in herself, never seeming to look back to that evening when she was miserable and close to falling off that rock on the cliff-top.

Mum hasn't said a thing about moving house lately. We're staying at Bondi, that's for sure.

Dad is on a late shift today, so he's up there leaning on the railings, watching me from the shade of the pines. Today is lit up with sunshine just as brilliant as the first day we came to live at the beach.

I hoist my board, fin uppermost, on to my head. The hot sand burns my feet as I stride towards the surf.

Down where the sand is smooth and saturated by the fingers of the ocean I pause for a few moments. I breathe the good air. I turn my head to look back at my father, and at the mounds of green grass beyond the railings, and at the graceful outlines of the trees against the rich blue of the sky.

The breeze blows from the shore, and the surf is hollow this morning. There's magic everywhere around the beach. It's a privilege to be alive.

There are other board riders around, some experts, some learners. At one time I would have curled up in self-conscious horror if I had thought there was anyone I knew around. Now I no longer care. Every surfer is a kind of companion. This, in my leisure time, is where I belong. It is where I am accepted, where everybody can be accepted, speaking the common language of surf people. There's a language for everybody in this country—it's just a matter of discovering what your own thing really is, then going out and doing it.

I try not to rush things. First I stay in the white water, ready to grab a good shore break. Paddling practice, then a gentle curving ride back to the edge of the beach.

More paddling practice, then more rides on the shore breaks.

My golden surfboard glints in the blinding sunlight. I can trust it all the way, and it seems like a live thing under me, trusting my guidance in the boiling white water.

Well, here goes. I'm off again, paddling way out beyond the broken surf this time. At last I lose myself in a string of board riders, all different abilities, all waiting for just the right wave to come looking up.

At last I pick out what seems to be a promising swell, heaving its way in our direction. I decide that this is a wave for me to catch. Straddling my board, I swing it round with unexpected ease—then I begin to paddle hard and the board is moving towards the beach. Somehow I've got it exactly right.

The rising wave is almost on me.

I paddle harder.

It breaks just a stroke or two behind me, and the sight of the sharp, overhanging edge on top makes the excitement rise inside me. I'm paddling like a mad thing, trying to catch the surge of the wave just right, praying it's not going to be a dumper.

Luck is riding tandem with me today. I have managed to time things right. Now the wave is doing the work and I feel the board surging forward.

I stop paddling and raise my chest a bit, gulping in air as I race forward. Somehow I manage to kneel without spoiling the trim of the board. I feel bolder. I scuttle to my feet, and the wax gives them a good grip.

It's unbelievable. My feet are positioned well and I'm steady on my lateral course. Hardly a muscle moves, and I resist the temptation to try a cut-back or some other stunt.

It feels like a dream.

Better than a dream.

But another surfie comes hot-dogging across my course, trying a cut-back turn that really just isn't on. He yells something at me.

I want to shout: 'Hey, get off my wave.' But I daren't take a breath to shout. Speechless, I am.

The other bloke's board nosedives and he is wiped out. His flailing body is in front of me, and his board is flung all over the place.

This looks like the end of my ride. I bend low and touch the rail with the finger tips of my left hand. I miss the board by inches.

Somehow I keep riding.

Now I draw myself a little higher again, but not too high because I know it's best to keep my centre of gravity low. But in my mind I'm giant-sized, a true conqueror of the waves.

The shoreline looks closer. The wave is breaking up behind me. Still, miraculously, I move forward. And this is what it's all about . . . what I've worked and saved for . . . not just owning a board but having a great ride on it, my only proper ride so far. It's better than the Cakewalk, the Big Wheel, and the Big Dipper all rolled into one.

It's better than a slide down the mountains of the moon.

At last I come riding clear up to the beach. When I transfer my weight to the back of the board I make it stall, then I slip into the water with scarcely

a splash. The board is within reach so I don't have the embarrassment of needing to chase it.

So far as I can tell, no one has been watching this ride. None of my mates can have seen the way I have conquered this part of the ocean. I don't care. What matters is that at last I'm really part of it all—the beach, the sky, the waves.

Maybe there are many other beaches waiting for me to surf them. Some of them, like Angourie or Waimea, are rated better than Bondi by the kings of the surfboards. So what if they are? This is a day when nobody could convince me of their superior wonders.

Bondi is good enough for me. It is here that I

will work at my surfing. Here, some day, I will be hot-dogging around—doing backhand cut-back turns, hanging five, or maybe even hanging ten.

Perhaps I'll be a surf champion of the future.

Perhaps not.

Now Sam, there's a bloke with the makings of a champion, on that bike of his. He's the one with the fierce competitive spirit, the will to win.

But Greg Stevens, goofy-footer, becoming a surf champion—that's a big think away.

Just for the present, I'm content to turn my board around and then paddle out to the zone beyond the white water, where the waves are being shaped.

Millions of other waves are going to come rolling into Bondi Beach from the wide ocean. Every wave is different, and some of them will belong to me.

IF YOU HAVE ENJOYED THIS BOOK
YOU MAY ALSO LIKE THESE

THE BLACK PEARL *by Scott O'Dell*   20p
552 52008 X   Carousel Fiction

The Black Pearl belonged to the old men, with legends and stories to
tell to pass the time—or so Ramon Salazar had thought, until he came
face to face with the devilfish and the struggle for the pearl began. But
Ramon had more than the dangers of the sea to conquer. Others
wanted the Great Pearl of Heaven, including the evil Pearler from
Seville.

THE MODEL-RAILWAY MEN *by Ray Pope*   25p
552 52024 1

Mark operates his model railway as near to the real thing as possible.
Then he encounters the Telford family, miniature people who live only
for the railway—Mark's railway. The adventures of Mark and his live
passengers will be enjoyed by anyone who has known the delights of a
model railway.

THE CLASHING ROCKS *by Ian Serraillier*   20p
552 52022 5

Ian Serraillier tells the story of Jason and the Argonauts, and of their
quest in search of the golden fleece. Jason and his crew sailed from
Thessaly to the Black Sea, encountering many of the daunting figures
from Greek mythology. This is the world of classical Greece, full of
demons and gods, and in Ian Serraillier's hands the timeless story is both
a great myth and a gripping adventure story.

TRUE MYSTERIES *by Robert Hoare*   25p

552 54009 9   Carousel Non-Fiction

Tales of the unknown, stories of people who suddenly appear and dis-
appear without explanation, and strange events which present no
logical answer, sometimes turning legend into fact, or fact into legend.
And always leaving a question mark.

20TH CENTURY DISCOVERY: 25p
THE STRUCTURE OF LIFE *by Isaac Asimov*

552 54012 9   Carousel Non-Fiction

20TH CENTURY DISCOVERY: THE PLANETS 25p
by Isaac Asimov

552 54013 7   Carousel Non-Fiction

Dr. Asimov's books recount the major events of scientific discovery in
this century: how the atom has been investigated and its power har-
nessed; how delicate the balance of nature is: and how, through his
examination of the structure of life, man may have come close to the
artificial creation of life itself; how the development of different tele-
scopes has enabled man to observe the stars and planets, how he has
calculated their age and distance, and how the development of space
travel has affected our knowledge of the Universe.
Illustrated with photographs.

THE STORY OF JODRELL BANK   30p
by Roger Piper

552 54028 5

We now live in the space age, and Jodrell Bank stands as one of the
greatest achievements of stellar technology. Here is the whole story of
the 'Big Dish', including its history, how it works, and some of the
amazing facts discovered by this modern wonder of the world. Also
included are eight pages of photographs.

All these books are available at your bookshop or newsagent or can be
ordered direct from **TRANSWORLD PUBLISHERS**. Just tick the
titles you want and fill in the form below.

TRANSWORLD PUBLISHERS. Cash Sales Department, P.O. Box
11, Falmouth, Cornwall.
Please send cheque or postal order—no currency, and allow 6p per
book to cover the cost of postage and packing.

NAME ....

ADDRESS...

(MARCH/73) ....